SAVAGE
KNIGHTS

PRINCES OF DEVIL'S CREEK BOOK THREE

JILLIAN FROST

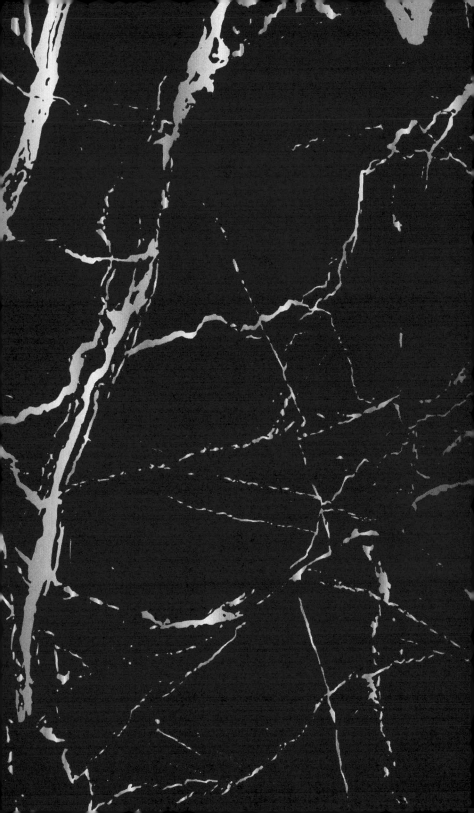

SAVAGE KNIGHTS

PRINCES OF DEVIL'S CREEK BOOK THREE

JILLIAN FROST

Also by Jillian Frost

Princes of Devil's Creek

Cruel Princes

Vicious Queen

Savage Knights

Battle King

Boardwalk Mafia

Boardwalk Kings

Boardwalk Queen

Boardwalk Reign

Devil's Creek Standalone Novels

The Darkest Prince

Wicked Union

For a complete list of books, visit JillianFrost.com.

This book is a work of fiction. Names, characters, places, and incidents are the product of the author's imagination or used fictitiously. Any resemblance to actual persons, both living or deceased, establishments, businesses, events, or locales is entirely coincidental.

SAVAGE KNIGHTS

PRINCES OF DEVIL'S CREEK BOOK THREE

JILLIAN FROST

Chapter One

LUCA

W e stood inside the vault and chose a crown for our queen—only the best for the future Mrs. Salvatore. I never thought we'd reach this point in our relationship. But everything was falling into place, the pieces moving across the board like a well-played game of chess.

Marcello opened a silk-lined box for me to place the crown inside. My great grandfather had stolen this crown from Italian nobility when he took the Salvatore diamond.

"It's perfect." A grin stretched the corners of Marcello's mouth. "Alex will love it."

I smiled, a rare one that touched my eyes. She was changing me, making me want to be a different man. An effect she had on all of us.

"She agreed to marry me."

"Marry us," Marcello corrected.

"And she's pregnant." My face hurt from smiling so hard. "Your plan worked. We'll satisfy the deal with The Founders Society."

"Told you it would work. I know Alex better than all of you combined." He leaned against the wall, arms folded with a know-it-all expression on his face. "She's told me from the start that it has to be all or none of us. But you were too stubborn to listen."

"Yeah." I nodded in agreement. "But I didn't think she would want to marry all four of us."

"Next time, listen to me, brother. I understand her in ways none of you ever will."

"That's why this works." I snapped the box shut and took the crown from his hands. "Between us, we'll make one decent husband."

Marcello tipped his head back and laughed. "Speak for yourself. Bash and I are not the ones with intimacy issues. I would have married Alex years ago if it were up to me."

I rolled my eyes at the fucking bastard. "Because you've been pining over her like some lovesick teenager."

He snickered. "Fuck you. Don't tell me you're not in love with her." When I didn't argue, he added, "Did you ever think someone could fix Damian? Look at him. He's different with her. So are you, Luca. You love her. Deal with it. Learn how to process your emotions like a normal human being."

I laughed at his suggestion. "Normal? What the fuck would any of us know about that?"

"You know what I mean." He patted me on the shoulder. "She's carrying one of our children. Soon, she'll be our wife and the Queen of The Devil's Knights. At some point, you'll realize you love her and say the words. And when you do, you'll have her forever. It's the one thing she wants from you. To hear you say it."

"Is that what you did?"

He rolled his broad shoulders. "I didn't have to tell her. She already knew I loved her. I showed her with my actions."

I scoffed at his comment. "And I haven't shown her? Please. There's nothing I wouldn't do for Alex."

He smirked. "Tell her how you feel before the wedding. It will mean a lot to her."

I turned away from him, overloaded by all the fucking feelings in the room. He was right about Alex. She wanted more intimacy, more love, more of anything I could give her.

For years, she waited for me to show her an ounce of affection. But I wasn't like Bastian and Marcello. They weren't as fucked up as Damian and me. So it was harder for them to understand why we were like this.

"We should go," Marcello suggested. "They're probably waiting for us in Alex's bedroom."

The steel walls of the vault glittered from all the jewels shimmering under the fluorescent lights. Hundreds of stolen pieces from around the world. Some belonged to nobles, while others we'd won or traded for debts owed to The Devil's Knights. A few pieces were in our possession until our clients could retrieve them.

We lent money to our clients and occasionally held valuables for them. Sometimes, we used our team of mercenaries, led by Marcello, to collect items. And in even more rare cases, to collect someone.

I stopped in front of a row of earrings that hung from a black velvet earring display. "One more piece."

I grabbed a pair of diamond and ruby drop earrings, placed them in a box, and stuffed them into my pocket. Then I glanced across the room at the necklaces. I pointed at the one that matched the crown and earrings. "Grab the necklace. She needs a matching set."

"So particular," he deadpanned as he removed the necklace from the collection and closed the lid.

I liked to plan everything, even Alex's wardrobe. Every piece of clothing and jewelry she owned was hand-selected by me. My brothers could have cared less. They didn't have my specific tastes.

After leaving the vault, I sealed it shut and stood in front of the retinal scanner. Then I pressed my hand to the screen on the wall. Only a Salvatore could access the vault, which required a two-step verification. Alex would learn our family secrets after the wedding. That was my father's one rule I would not break. He didn't let anyone outside of our family have access to any of our secrets.

On our way down the narrow hallway, my cell phone dinged with several missed calls from Bastian. I turned to look at my brother. "Did Bash call you?"

He checked his cell phone and shook his head. "No, why? Is something wrong?"

"I don't know." I stuffed the phone into my pocket and ascended the stairs leading to the secret passage. "He called a few times in a row. That's not like him."

I stopped at the top landing and glanced down a few steps at Marcello. "Why would they lock the door when we were right behind them?"

A worried look crossed his face as he reached for his gun. I kept my gun at my side as I unlatched the lock and pushed on the door connected to the bookcase.

Inside the library, it was dark and quiet. I liked this side of the house for that reason. It was easier to think with all the silence.

When I was a boy, I spent hours each day in the library. While inside this room, I didn't hear the voices in my head telling me to be more like my father, urging me to keep sinning.

This room was my sanctuary.

Marcello followed me into the library. At first, nothing looked out of place. Not until I spotted Bastian passed out on the floor a few feet from Damian. I dropped to my knees beside Bastian and checked his pulse. He was still breathing. Then I repeated the same process with Damian. They were unconscious but alive.

What the fuck happened?

I shot up from the floor and glanced around the room. "Where the fuck is Alex?"

"Already on it." Marcello flipped through his cell phone

and gasped when he stopped on a particular clip of security footage. "Savanna Wellington."

She wasn't a Wellington anymore. Carl had disowned the bitch after she left my father, ran away from Devil's Creek, and married Alex's dad to spite her family.

My heart thudded in my chest as I looked over Marcello's shoulder at the footage. A tall man with dark hair jammed a needle into Alex's neck. She staggered to the side, clutching her neck, and then Savanna appeared.

"Play that back." I pointed at the screen. "And turn up the volume. What is Savanna saying to Alex?"

He replayed the video.

A man stepped out from the shadows in the room's corner and injected Damian with a sedative. He muttered something and hit the floor like a sack of bricks, out cold.

Alex spun around to look at Damian. Bastian pointed his gun at an assailant. Another man moved so quickly I didn't see him coming, and neither did my brother. The man knocked the gun from Bastian's hand and stabbed him with a syringe. Before he knew what was happening, his head hit the floor.

Alex screamed.

The injection they'd given her wasn't as strong as my brothers. She was still on her feet, swaying to the side as her bitch mother moved toward her.

She looked like Alex's older twin with the same curly hair, pouty pink lips, and curves hugged a tight black dress. I used to confuse Alex for her mother when we were younger. Until recently, I saw Savanna whenever I looked at Alex. But she was nothing like her mother. Unfortunately, it took me too long to see that.

I looked at Marcello, eyes narrowed. "How did she get into Devil's Creek without us knowing? She hasn't come back here in over thirty years. Why now?"

"She wants the bounty."

He hit play on the video, and Savanna started talking to Alex.

"Hello, darling." She twirled a blonde curl around her painted fingernail and smiled. "Did you miss me?"

"How?" Alex muttered, blinking in rapid succession.

"It's not how you should be asking." A wicked glint flared in her blue eyes as she held her daughter's gaze. "It's why."

Alex's lips parted to speak, but she lost her balance before she could get out another word. Her mother's arm shot out to catch her. She passed her to the men beside her. "Get her in the car."

One man lifted Alex and left the library through the secret passage. The other followed him with his gun in hand. *How could they have known how long we would be in the vault? She'd only brought three men with her. Had I not stopped to get the crown, the five of us would have been together. There was no way they would have subdued all of us.*

"Fuck," I groaned. "This is my fault. I shouldn't have deviated from our plan."

Savanna flicked her hair over her shoulder and leaned into a man in his late forties that wasn't her husband. He had dark hair, dressed in a tailored black suit. She kissed his lips and then dragged him to the exit door. The bookcase closed over the passage, and they were gone.

Marcello scanned the cameras in the catacombs. Without looking, I knew how they got in and out of our estate. As the only daughter of a Founder, Savanna was privy to the secret passages which connected all the estates on Founders Way.

They were supposed to be used in emergencies to help each other. The Wellingtons had taken a lot from my family.

Savanna, most of all.

My blood boiled as I watched Marcello check each of the security feeds. They ran down the beach behind the man who carried a passed-out Alex. Then they got into a boat at the far end of the beach, on the other side of the bay.

I gritted my teeth, fists clenched at my sides. "She's fucking dead when I find her."

Marcello grunted in agreement. "Savanna thinks she outsmarted us." He shoved the phone into his pocket. "She doesn't know Alex is wearing the Salvatore diamond."

"We can track her." I tapped him on the back. "Wake up Damian and Bash." With my back to him, I moved toward the exit doors. "Tell Drake to track Alex's location while I prepare the Knights for deployment."

Chapter Two

MARCELLO

Pacing back and forth across the helipad, I gritted my teeth. How could I let them take her? As the head of security, it was my job to see the flaws in every plan and assess every situation. So far, our enemies had outmaneuvered us at every turn.

We couldn't plan anymore, not with most men from the criminal underworld vying for the bounty.

Alex was gone.

I felt completely out of control for the first time in my life. I was always the calm brother, even when tested to the limits. Like a diamond, I would never crack under pressure. Years of training with Alpha Command had prepared me for anything. But I'd never considered the possibility of losing Alex.

I failed her.

Failed my family.

Knowing I put Alex in this situation shut down every sensible part of my brain. Without Alex to level me out, I was ready to explode from all the rage bubbling inside me.

Luca cupped my shoulder, snapping my attention back to reality. "We'll find her. Give it time."

"They will sell her to the highest bidder."

"Savanna wants the bounty," Luca said with certainty. "She'll hand Alex off and go on her way."

"I know what Savanna wants." I shoved his hand off my shoulder, not wanting to be touched. "The people she's working with are a wild card."

"If they want the bounty, they have to keep her alive until the auction."

"We don't know the motivations of the people she's working with," I said with a hint of anger in my tone, not meant for my brother. "What if this is about revenge? What if the person who bought her only wanted to torture and kill her to hurt us?"

The sickos in our world never kept women alive for long. They either hurt them so badly that they died from their injuries or put them out of their misery. The organizers of the private auctions didn't reveal the buyers' identities. So we had one option—find Alex before they moved her to the Il Circo location.

My fingers itched as I waited for a text message with the details. They didn't hold auctions in the same place more than once, making it harder for us to anticipate their next move. All the Knights had placed bids to give us the auction location.

"Don't blame yourself for this, Marcello. None of us saw Savanna coming." Luca leaned into my arm, throwing some of his weight into me. "I spoke with Carl. He forced Savanna to hand over her key when he disowned her thirty years ago." He rolled his shoulders, a perplexed expression on his face. "I don't know how she did it, but I guess she made a copy of the key."

You couldn't walk into a hardware store and have the skeleton key reproduced. So she must have found someone who specialized in the art of key making. Someone who could create a mold and melt down the brass to form the correct shape.

I nodded. "Yeah, but... I still feel responsible. She would still be with us if we hadn't stopped at the vault."

"Then blame me." Luca took a deep breath and turned his head away, staring at the far end of the helipad. "I asked you to accompany me to the vault."

There was no point in going back and forth with my brother. We both felt guilty. It was too late to talk about what we should or shouldn't have done.

The only way out is through.

The local Knights gathered on the helipad at my estate, waiting for Luca to issue an order. Carl Wellington stood beside my father and shot me a stern look. The Wellingtons had every reason to blame us. We had made a promise to protect our queen at all costs.

Sonny and Drake stopped in front of me. Drake was busy typing on the iPad in his hand.

"I located the Basiles' shipping container." Sonny chewed on his lip. "We didn't understand why their container was the only one that disappeared. Now it all makes sense."

Before I got shot, someone had stolen the Basiles container while it was in transit to the port. The Knights had met with Carl the day we discovered the theft. We handled illegal shipments for the Basile crime family monthly. The Russian ambush was convenient timing because the container went off our radar the same day.

I looked at Sonny for answers. "What did you find in the container?"

Drake held out the iPad. "You'll want to see this."

My brother leaned over my shoulder to look at the screen. The man in the video walked into the empty shipping container and ripped a white piece of paper off the wall.

Luca stiffened beside me.

He unfolded the paper and held it up to the camera for us to see. Luca gasped as he read the handwritten note. My heart raced so quickly that my pulse pounded in my ears, beating so loudly I could hardly hear my brother speaking to me.

"They stole their own container," I said in disbelief.

Luca nodded. "The fifteenth anniversary of mom's death is coming up. Lorenzo Basile has waited a long time to get revenge."

"He was waiting for Alex to take her place with the Knights."

"Aiden, too." Luca's jaw clenched as he looked at me. Then he turned to Sonny and Drake. "Does Wellington know yet?"

They shook their heads in unison.

"With both of his pawns out of play, maybe he'll get off his ass and offer us the help of The Founders Society."

Luca pushed past them and headed straight to Carl Wellington. I stayed behind and took the iPad from Drake's hand to reread the note.

We captured your Queen.
Took your Knight.
Make your move.

Chapter Three

ALEX

I rolled back and forth on a hard surface, struggling to break free from the ties binding my arms behind my back. Compared to Bastian and Damian's creative methods during sex, the restraints were nothing. I knew how to handle pain, something my men had taught me well.

I felt the diamond ring on my finger, surprised my mother hadn't taken it. She was a greedy bitch who would have done anything to make a quick buck. My parents couldn't hold down decent jobs and rarely worked because they were waiting around for their big break. They were both artists and not very good ones.

I knew why she took me.

The bitch wanted the bounty on my head. People from the depths of the criminal underworld wanted to collect.

How did she know about it?

I hadn't heard a word from her in over six years. Not since the day my grandfather came to the house with a team of armed men and removed Aiden and me from her home. From that day forward, we were no longer Aiden and Alexandrea Fox.

We became Wellingtons.

Rich and powerful and with targets on our heads. Our lives hadn't been the same since, but it beat the alternative. With our parents, we didn't have a life.

We just survived.

I inched the diamond ring down my finger, trying to keep a firm hold on it. It was the only reminder I had of my men. They would come for me. The Salvatore brothers would burn down the world and everyone in it for their queen.

I stuffed the ring into my back pocket. It was the one thing I would never let my mother take from me. She had tried to strip me of my self-esteem and my sanity growing up. Every day with her felt like my own version of Hell.

Locked closets.

Dark rooms.

My screams.

Her laughter.

A nagging pain stabbed the side of my head, pounding from the lingering effects of the drugs and the migraine penetrating my skull. Images of the past flashed through my mind, like a highlight reel of all my pain and suffering. She never cared about me, never loved me like a real mother. I was nothing more than a bargaining chip she held over my grandfather's head.

I still couldn't believe she tried to use my sketches to get my grandfather to let her back into his life. To regain the fortune she had lost. My entire life, she treated me worse than trash and tormented me when she didn't get her way with my grandfather. The truth made me sick to my stomach.

She killed my idol.

Stole a mother from her children.

A wife from her husband.

Years of suffering and beatings and torture my men received from their father. All because he was hurting over the death of Evangeline. Because he was so madly in love with his wife that losing her destroyed him.

His sons almost did the same to me.

A cloth that smelled like smoke covered my mouth. The scent was so overpowering it made my stomach churn, creating a nasty taste in the back of my throat. My morning sickness had been taking its toll on my body. A wave of nausea smacked me in the face.

I was pregnant.

And they drugged me.

I said a silent prayer the baby would be okay and that no harm would come to them. I wasn't ready to be a mother, but I wanted this baby.

Blinking a few times, I refocused my gaze and saw nothing but black. We were moving, the space dark and cramped. After escaping The Mansion, I was growing more accustomed to the dark. It didn't scare me as much as before my men tested the limits of my mental illness.

My head pounded like a jackhammer drilling into concrete. Waves of nausea washed over me every time I rocked from side to side. Both of my shoulders hurt. They must have thrown me into the trunk like an old gym bag. Not a second thought that I was a living, breathing human being.

Luca told me pain is weakness leaving the body, a lesson he learned from his father. As I let his words wash over me, I thought about his rough touch and strong hands that had brought me to the brink of insanity for years. Being with my men had prepared me in different ways.

I prayed my handsome devils would find me. That they would gather The Devil's Knights and not stop searching for me.

When the car stopped, I closed my eyes, pretending to sleep. I had no way of freeing myself from the restraints. It was better if they thought I was still unconscious. Then maybe I could use my senses to figure out where they were taking me.

The trunk opened. Saltwater penetrated my nostrils. Waves crashed from a distance.

One man reached into the trunk and lifted me over his shoulder. He held me against his hard chest and smacked my ass. I ignored the pain, which shot up my leg, and pretended to sleep.

We moved closer to the water.

From what I could tell, we were at a marina. Fishing boats and yachts surrounded a large pier.

My heart slammed into my chest, the adrenaline and fear taking over. If we were traveling by water, how would they find me? Tears stung my eyes as he dropped me to the ground like a bag of garbage.

I groaned as my shoulder hit the wooden planks. Overcome by an intense pain traveling down to my lower back, settling into my bones, I cried out. But the handkerchief muffled the sound.

"She's awake," a man said in a thick Italian accent.

My heart clambered out of my chest, beating so hard and fast that my head spun. I struggled to catch my breath with the cloth over my mouth. The disgusting smell didn't help.

A million horrible thoughts raced through my head as a boat approached the pier. They were going to sell me at Il Circo, the online auction where anything goes. But I had faith my men would stop their enemies.

A phone rang, cutting through the noise of the yacht's engine. The man beside me raised the phone to his ear, his voice husky and with what sounded like a New York accent.

Who the hell are these people?

"They're offering twenty-five million?"

"Tell them to make it fifty," my mother hissed in an arrogant tone, "and we have a deal."

A shiver rushed down my spine.

Fifty million dollars?

If she wanted money, my men would have given it to her without the drama. She didn't have to go to these lengths to fuck with my life. My grandfather wouldn't have budged. He would have held his ground and forced her hand.

Maybe that was why I was here. This was her way of showing my grandfather that no matter how much wealth and power he had gained, she could take it from him.

My thoughts drifted to Aiden. I wasn't the only heir to the Wellington fortune. Aiden was the heir apparent to take over for my grandfather after his retirement. He had the most to lose and everything to gain.

So why didn't she go for him?

Or did she?

The thought of anyone hurting my twin brother twisted my stomach into knots. Aiden was a free spirit, an artist who wasn't fit to join the ranks of The Devil's Knights.

Aiden.

He better be okay.

When I closed my eyes, I listened to the waves.

Luca loved the sea.

So did Marcello.

They could have lived on a boat if they didn't have the weight of the world pressing down on their shoulders. The sound, the smell, everything about the sea reminded me of my handsome devils. I envisioned my savage Knights coming to my rescue.

It was only a matter of time.

With my ankles bound, my legs hit the man's back with each step we took toward the boat. His shoes slapped the wooden planks, with multiple sets of footsteps following us.

"About time," a man in front of us shouted. "We're leaving in ten." He cleared his throat as we approached the yacht. "The Salvatores got their invitation to the island. So have The Devil's Knights. All of their known associates will be in attendance for the wedding."

What wedding?

"They've gotten in our way long enough," another man said in a thick Italian accent.

"Throw her in," a man growled.

Into the water?

His words caused me to panic. With the fabric covering my mouth, I couldn't breathe.

We walked onto the yacht that smelled of raw fish and saltwater. I heard my mother scream, her voice not far behind me.

"No!" she yelled. "We had a deal, you idiot. Put me down! Do you have any idea who I am?"

A man laughed. "You served your purpose, bitch."

The man holding me turned to the left, away from my mother's screams, and led me down a long hallway.

They decorated the walls with expensive paintings, and as we passed the saloon, I spotted an original Evangeline Franco painting hung on the wall above a mantle.

My captor stopped in front of a door at the end of the corridor. He stepped into the room and lowered me onto a mattress on the floor. My shoulder broke the fall, and a searing pain shot down my arm. Every bone in my body hurt from the drugs and lack of sleep. A red-hot blaze licked my skin, creating a dangerous fire I couldn't contain.

A man slept on the mattress beside me with his head turned to the side. I scooted closer to look at his blond curly hair and gasped.

"Aiden!" I shook his shoulder. "Aiden, wake up!"

Is he dead?

"Shut up!" The Italian man hunched down so I could feel his breath on my cheek. "It's time to take your medicine."

He jammed a needle into my neck.

Once again, I felt myself detaching from reality, slowly losing consciousness.

And then, nothing.

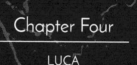

Chapter Four

LUCA

The vein in my neck throbbed with each breath I took. I walked over to Carl Wellington, repeating the words from the note in my head.

We captured your Queen.
Took your Knight.
Make your move.

Lorenzo Basile thought he was clever. But a knight in chess could jump over any piece, regardless of color, and capture their enemy, wiping them from the board.

Aiden was too valuable to them.

They wouldn't kill him, though they probably would torture him until he wished he were dead. So it all made sense why the Basiles forced my father to work with them. They were playing the long game. Fifteen years to plan their revenge for a crime Alex and Aiden didn't commit.

My great uncle didn't need the money. The Basiles had controlled Southern Italy for fifty years and had amassed enough wealth and power to topple a small country.

A part of me wanted to rub the situation in Carl's smug fucking face. He refused to offer the Knights more help when we begged him for it.

We took Aiden under our wings, brought him into The Devil's Knights, and trained him to become one of us. He was only a few months into his initiation. I still couldn't wrap my head around how the Sicilians had gotten to Aiden without the Knights knowing about it.

For the past month, he'd been living in a secure off-grid location. Only the higher-ranking Knights knew about the safe house.

So how did they find him?

They had outsmarted us at every turn and blocked our attempts to get out from under this situation. I wondered if they were working with the Russians, even though they had been enemies for years. But now, they had a common enemy.

"The Basiles have taken Alex and Aiden," I told Carl.

His head snapped to me, and his nostrils flared. "Are you certain?"

I nodded, then repeated the exact words of the note our men had found in the empty shipping container. We thought it was strange the Basiles container was the only one missing from the carrier. And for it to disappear mid-transit was even more bizarre.

"I contacted Aiden's Pledge Master. Missing video surveillance confirms they kidnapped him from the safe house around the same time Savanna took Alex. He's gone."

My father aimed his stern expression at me. "How did this happen? Only a handful of men knew the location of the safe house."

"I don't think it's corruption within the Knights," I assured him.

"No?" Carl's eyebrows rose a half-inch. "Because it sounds like you can't control your men."

"This wasn't the Knights," my dad said in our defense.

"There will be an investigation into every man at the safe house." Carl clenched his jaw as he aimed his hardened gaze at me. "I blame you. If you weren't such a spoiled brat, you would have put your pride aside a long ago and made this work with my granddaughter. I didn't have to agree to this marriage. I didn't have to make this right."

"It's my fault." I nodded in agreement. "I should have done a lot of things. But it's too late to dwell on the past."

"Do you have Alex's location?" Carl asked.

I bobbed my head to confirm. "Drake is coordinating with the pilot as we speak."

A long beat of silence passed between us, with nothing more than the sound of the chopper's blades rotating, filling the air. Everyone was on edge. Even Marcello, who was always in control, looked ready to jump out of his skin.

Damian and Bastian were still feeling the effects of the drugs and not quite themselves. They leaned against each other by the helicopter.

"Lorenzo is going to marry Alex," I said without a single doubt in my mind. "That's what I would do."

If we didn't find her in time, she would have to marry a Mafia Don. Lorenzo Basile was my great uncle and the leader of the family in Calabria. My mother's parents had fled from Italy to get away from the violence. They made the right choice, but my mom never got away from them.

Carl scrubbed a hand across his jaw. "How does he know about the dowry? That's not information I share with outsiders."

"My mother was close with Lorenzo," I pointed out. "She was his favorite niece. Maybe she mentioned it to him."

"No." Dad shook his head. "Your mother knew better than to discuss our business with the Basiles."

I rolled my shoulders. "I guess we'll never know."

I considered myself a patient man. I'd waited years to claim Alex. To get her back, I had to exercise the same patience. One wrong move and I would never see her again.

Drake crossed the helipad with Marcello and Sonny at his

sides. He looked determined, walking with a purpose as he strode toward me with the iPad.

He shoved the screen in front of me. "They're on the move again."

Carl and my father leaned over me to get a better look. A man carried Alex toward a yacht, and two more men dressed in dark suits followed. He dropped her onto the dock as if she were insignificant. Alex's eyes slightly opened as she struggled against her restraints, the ties binding her arms and legs.

I pointed at a dark-haired man with a scar that ran down the length of his neck. "I know him. He's a Capo in the Basile crime family."

"I didn't see Lorenzo anywhere on the feeds," Drake said.

"He'll be at the final destination," Marcello interjected.

"What about Aiden?" Sonny asked.

Drake nodded. "He'll be there, too."

Carl held my gaze for a moment with a menacing glare in his eyes. "You better find my grandchildren. If any harm comes to them, you will pay the price."

Chapter Five

ALEX

I woke up to the sound of water splashing the side of the boat. Thunder boomed so loudly that my heart raced at the bolts striking the water. I rolled onto my side, surprised to find my hands and legs free from the restraints.

I glanced around the room in search of water. My tongue stuck to the roof of my mouth, lips chapped and cracked from dehydration. The disgusting taste of bile crept up the back of my throat.

I clutched my stomach and fought the wave of nausea and the stabbing pains in my stomach. I squeezed my eyes shut, desperate to make the pain go away. But, I could barely move an inch between the migraine working its way to the back of my head and the sickness washing over me.

Someone tapped me on the shoulder. "Lexie, wake up."

Aiden.

I blinked a few times, attempting to focus on my twin brother's face, which looked slightly blurred at the edges. Was he real or a figment of my imagination? It wouldn't have been the first time I saw his face when he wasn't here.

I pinched the skin on my arm to see if it hurt.

Not dreaming.

There was no way my brother was here. And yet, when I reached up to cup his cheek with my hand, his warmth rushed through my fingertips.

"You're real?" I whispered.

He clutched my wrist and smiled. "I'm real, Lexie."

I tried to sit up and nearly fell over from all the drugs. Until now, I'd never done a single drug. I didn't know what it felt like to be high. It was an awful feeling I never wanted to experience again.

Aiden propped me up against the wall beside him. He pressed his palm to my forehead and sighed. "How are you feeling?"

"Like someone drugged me," I choked out, my voice hoarse. "Why are you here?"

"Because of Pops," he said through clenched teeth. "That would be my guess. His stupid money and that deal he made with the Salvatores."

"We're not here because of them."

He shook his head, his blond curls falling into his face. It was longer than the last time I saw him. "We should have run a long time ago, Lexie. You don't owe Pops for the rest of your life. I will find a way off this boat."

"We'll never be free, Aid."

"I will die trying to make that happen," he shot back.

"I'm glad you're here." I laid my head on his shoulder, accepting our fate for the moment. "But I wish you didn't have to be involved."

"I'm the only male heir to the Wellington fortune," he said with irritation in his tone. "They want to use me as leverage against Pops."

"Where are we?"

He looked down at me. "On a boat with a bunch of Italians."

I rubbed my temples and sighed. "Yeah, but where are we going?"

He rolled his broad shoulders against the wall. "I don't know. Men kidnapped me from a safe house in the middle of the night. They knocked me out cold." My twin shoved my curls behind my ears and studied my face. "I knew we shouldn't have trusted the Salvatores. They promised to keep you safe if I joined The Devil's Knights."

"You can't blame them for every bad thing that happens to me," I told him. "Mom kidnapped me."

He gasped at my confession. "Mom?"

I nodded, still in disbelief that my mother was behind my forced captivity. "She spoke to me before the drugs knocked me out."

His eyes narrowed. "What did she say?"

"I asked her how she got inside the Salvatore Estate. And she said the question I should have asked is why."

"That greedy fucking bitch." His jaw flexed as he looked at me. "She wants the bounty. So when the person who listed you at the last auction didn't produce you, the bounty raised to four million dollars. Then it increased to five."

I slumped to the side, using my brother's weight to support me. "Yeah, I worked that much out for myself. The man she was with said they offered twenty-five million. And then, she told him to up it to fifty million."

He slung his arm around me. "It's going to be okay. I promise."

"At least there's a silver lining." A smile tipped up the corners of my mouth. "They screwed her over. I heard one of the Italian men drag her onto the boat. She was screaming about them having a deal, and he said she served her purpose."

His smile mirrored mine. "Good. That bitch will get what she deserves."

I forced myself to sit up, tucking my legs under my butt. "They invited the Salvatores and The Devil's Knights."

"They're holding the Il Circo auction on an island."

"Which one?"

"I don't know." Aiden shrugged. "The invites hadn't gone out before they kidnapped me." He pushed the hair off his forehead and expelled a breath of air from his lungs. "Mom didn't have to do this to you. I would have given her my trust fund just to get rid of her."

"She isn't working alone, Aid." I covered his hand with mine on the mattress. "They used the catacombs beneath the Salvatore Estate to get into the house. Only the Founders know about them."

He looked down at me, his blue eyes ringed with dark circles from exhaustion. "They used her for insider knowledge."

We sat silent for a while, still trying to wrap our heads around the situation. I hadn't seen my twin in months, and it felt good to have him by my side.

I didn't know what these people wanted from either of us. It had to be about more than money.

"How long have you been here?" I tilted my head to the side. "Has anyone come to check on you?"

He covered his mouth and yawned, looking as if he were seconds from falling asleep. "I woke up right before they brought you in here. And then they drugged me again."

"We have to get out of here." I got on my knees, grabbing his shoulder to maintain my balance. "I don't care if we have to jump overboard. Whatever these men have planned for us will not end well."

"The Knights will be at the island." Aiden slid his arm behind my back and helped me up from the mattress. We staggered to the side, still dizzy from the drugs. "They won't come to the auction without a plan."

"They said something about a wedding."

"Someone wants the Wellington dowry," he guessed.

"Yeah, but there's one small problem." I reached into my back pocket, relieved to find the diamond ring still there. "Aid,

I need to tell you something." I raised the massive diamond ring so he could see it. "I'm engaged."

His pale blue eyes widened. "You said yes to Luca?"

I gulped down my nerves and slid the ring onto my finger. "I said yes to all four of them."

"Excuse me?" His eyebrows knitted with confusion. "What do you mean, all four of them?"

"Exactly what I said. I'm in a relationship with Luca, Bastian, Marcello, and Damian."

Aiden ran his fingers through his messy curls and groaned. Unable to look at me, he breathed deeply through his nose. "I should have done more to get you away from them."

"Stop blaming yourself for everything that happens to me." I tugged on his bicep hard enough to gain his attention. "Aiden, I love them. I'm in love with all four of them."

His head snapped to me, his mouth twisted in disgust. "I asked Marcello to take care of you. Not to share you with his brothers like a fucking whore."

"It's not like that," I assured him, ignoring the sting of his last comment. "I know how it sounds. Four men and one woman."

"It sounds like a fucking porno," he snapped.

"Aiden, please." I curled my fingers around my arm. "Just listen to me."

His eyes found mine, though they were glassy and sadder than before. "Go on."

"I didn't mean for it to happen. But over the past few months, I've fallen in love with each of them. It's not just about sex."

"I'm not okay with this, Lexie." His nose scrunched as he mulled over my words. "Pops agreed to let one of them marry you, not all four. And they're brothers! That would be like you and me sharing a woman. It's fucking ridiculous."

"What do you want me to say?" I pushed my hands onto

my hips and glared at him. "I love them. I said yes. And for the record, two of them are not brothers."

"It's disgusting!" Aiden shook his head. "You're a Wellington, an heiress, not some cheap whore they can pass around for pleasure."

"Aiden, stop it! You're acting like an asshole."

My brother walked toward the window on the opposite side of the room. "You're my sister." He looked out the curtains and then angled his body to look at me. "My twin fucking sister." Aiden leaned against the wall and crossed his arms over his chest. "The thought of four men touching you sickens me. You deserve more. None of them are good enough for you."

"I have something else to tell you," I muttered, though I wasn't sure I had the heart to tell him anything else, not with how he was overreacting. "I'm pregnant."

With that, he stormed over to the door and turned the knob, pulling so hard I thought it would rip off.

"You can't run from me, Aiden."

He spun around to face me, cheeks flushed. "I'm not leaving you. I need to get you out of here."

"Did you hear what I said?" I rubbed my hand over my stomach. "I'm pregnant."

"Yeah." He pinched the bridge of his nose between his fingers and sighed. "I heard you. Who's the father?"

"I don't know." I strolled over to him, doing my best to stand on my own. "I found out I was pregnant the night Mom kidnapped me."

"I'm going to be an uncle?" Aiden's frown transformed into a bright smile. He scratched the blond stubble on his jaw. "I'll be back from initiation before you have the baby."

"If we get out of here alive," I said to state the obvious.

He groaned. "It won't be easy."

Footsteps pounded the floorboards outside of the room.

Then I heard a disturbance in the hall. Several men argued, their deep voices sending a chill down my spine.

Their footsteps moved closer.

So I stripped off the engagement ring and tucked it into my back pocket for safekeeping.

Aiden stepped back from the door.

And when it swung open, two men walked inside. The taller of the two pushed Aiden farther into the room and warned him to stand back. Of course, my brother swung at him, taking his best shot, one of which landed on the man's jaw.

The other man was shorter and had a scar on his cheek. He carried a tray of food that hit the floor. The taller man choked Aiden from behind. I screamed, and then the short guy advanced on me.

"You're not taking her!" Aiden shouted as he did his best to subdue his attacker.

My brother kicked and struggled, determined to break free. I screamed for them to stop. But it was too late. The man had choked my brother unconscious. He threw Aiden's limp body onto the mattress as if he weighed nothing.

I rushed over to him and checked his pulse.

"He's alive," the man assured me.

The taller man stood above me and offered his hand. I sneered at him. And when I didn't take his hand, he lifted me from the floor.

He pressed the barrel of a gun to my temple. "Start walking."

I gulped down the fear clawing up the back of my throat and followed his orders, taking one last look at my brother as they slammed the door.

With the other man behind us, we moved down a long hallway. The yacht was like a floating hotel, decorated in various shades of white and cream with expensive paintings hung on the walls. It surprised me to see some of my favorite artists. But when I spotted at least five original Evangeline Franco paintings, my mouth dropped in surprise.

We climbed the stairs to the next deck in silence. I didn't get cute with the man pointing a gun at the back of my head. I also didn't want them to hurt my brother or my baby. I had too much to lose, and they knew it.

At the end of the corridor, we halted before a closed door. A man knocked, and another man on the other side told him to come inside.

We entered the dinette. A handsome older man, dressed in a black suit, crisp white shirt, and a black tie, sat in an oversized armchair. He ran a hand through his short, black hair with a slight wave and smiled as he gazed at my body.

He held out his hand, gesturing at the table filled with plates. The mixture of garlic, steak, and fish hit my nostrils, and my stomach rumbled.

"Alexandrea," he said in a deep tone, his accent thick and Italian. "Join me for lunch."

Chapter Six

ALEX

I stared at the dark-haired man sitting across the table from me, sizing him up as he inspected every inch of my body. His intense gaze seared my skin, but not in the same way it did with my men. I felt like spiders were crawling up and down my arms.

Powerful men all had the same air about them. They sat with their shoulders squared and heads held high, a look of determination in their eyes. The Salvatore brothers had the same look. Much like the man before me, they oozed confidence by the truckload.

We held each other's gazes for a minute before he poured a glass of wine and slid it across the table.

"I can't drink alcohol," I told him, gulping down the nerves slithering up the back of my throat. "I need water."

He eyed me with curiosity. "Can't drink or don't want to?"

I shrugged. "Does it matter?"

He spoke Italian to a man who poured me a glass of water from a pitcher. I gave him a thankful nod and drank all of it.

I set the glass on the table and looked at the man across from me. "Why am I here?"

A soul-stealing smirk tipped up the corner of his mouth. "That's a long story."

I leaned back in the chair, crossed my arms over my chest, and held my ground. "I have the time."

He shoved a plate in front of me. Then he lifted two steak knives from the table and rubbed them together to intimidate me. "Eat, Alexandrea. You'll need your strength for the wedding."

I gripped my fork so hard that it left an indent in my palm. "What wedding?"

He smiled with his eyes and chewed his steak. "Our wedding."

My heart dropped into my stomach, and despite my hunger, I was no longer in the mood to eat. "I'm already engaged. I'm not marrying you."

His evil laughter filled the silence between us. "Not like you have a choice."

My entire body trembled from his confession. I kept the fork firmly gripped in my palm, just in case I needed to attack him.

"Who are you?"

He sliced into his steak and looked up from his plate. "Lorenzo Basile."

Fuck, no.

Now I understood why he had original Evangeline Franco paintings. Because she was his niece, and she painted them for him.

Which meant…

He wanted to marry me, so he could get his revenge. Marcello had mentioned the Basile family. They blamed the Salvatores for Evangeline's death.

Lorenzo flashed an evil grin. "I see you've heard of me."

I cleared my throat and sat straighter. "Marcello mentioned you," I said calmly. "He said you're his uncle."

"Great uncle," he corrected. "His mother was my niece."

Lorenzo looked too young to be Evangeline Franco's uncle. She would have been around fifty years old if she were still alive. So he couldn't have been more than a few years older than her, give or take.

"You don't have to fear me, Alexandrea." Lorenzo reached across the table and tapped a heavy gold and diamond ring on the side of my plate. "I didn't poison your food. Eat."

"Where are you taking me?"

"*Isola del Diavolo*," he said with a creepy grin.

I shoved a few pieces of steak into my mouth and spoke to him between bites. "Why are you doing this to me?"

Before he could answer, several pairs of shoes hit the floor in the hallway, moving slowly toward us. He shifted in his chair and glanced at the entryway as two men entered the room with my mother. They tied her wrists behind her back, and a bandana covered her mouth.

I grinned at the sight of her vulnerable and with no way out of this mess. Lorenzo tricked her into bringing me to him. Now, she had nothing to show for all of her schemes.

Stupid bitch.

Lorenzo rose from the chair and ripped the bandana from her mouth. My mother shouted one curse after the other. He slapped her face so hard that her eyes rolled back into her head.

A single tear slid down her cheek.

I'd never seen my mother back down to anyone. Instead, she steamrolled my father and exerted her power over Aiden and me. To see her scared, her limbs shaking with fear, filled me with a sick satisfaction.

She was always in control for my entire life—the one pulling the strings. I wished Aiden was here to see it for himself. To see the moment our mother had accepted defeat.

"You think you're so smart?" Lorenzo bent down to match her height, clutching her chin with his fingers.

"Thought you could hand over your daughter and walk away unscathed."

"I..." She tripped on her words, unable to finish her thought.

Did she not know Lorenzo Basile was Evangeline Franco's uncle? My mother was ruthless and had a black heart made of tar. She thought she could play a game with monsters because she was just like them.

I soaked up her fear like Damian savored a kill. It was too delicious seeing her tremble before a Mafia boss. The man who thought he would get me down the aisle.

That wasn't fucking happening.

Over my dead body.

"You killed my niece," Lorenzo said in a deep tone, his lips so close to hers they could have kissed. "You took her from this world. But death is too kind for you." He ran his thumb across her bottom lip and smirked. "You're taking your daughter's place at the auction tonight."

My lips parted.

Take that bitch!

My mother whimpered when he touched her again. This time, he wrapped his long fingers around her throat and squeezed.

"Please," she choked out. "My father is a powerful man. He will give you whatever you want."

"Your father disowned you thirty years ago. He hasn't spoken to you since." Lorenzo pointed his free hand at me. "Alexandrea and her brother are the heirs to the Wellington fortune. You're nothing more than a whore who flaunted herself at my men to make a quick buck."

"No, I didn't," she said in her defense. "I had a partnership with Sal. He said I could collect the money and walk away if I turned over my daughter."

Lorenzo refocused his gaze on her and clasped both hands around her throat, lifting her feet off the floor. "I have lined up the most depraved men to bid on you. They will break you mentally and physically. Suck the soul from your body and make you wish for death." He laughed in her face. "You will beg for the privilege of them ending your life. But they won't. For as long as I live, you will endure my wrath. Then, you will repent for your sins."

"I'm sorry," she choked out.

"Sorry doesn't cut it." He shook his head. "Not when you took my Eva from this world." Lorenzo released his hold on my mother and threw her at his men. "Do what you want with this whore. Get her out of my fucking sight."

My stomach churned at the thought of what they would do to her. And why did I even care? Why did I feel sick at the thought of men raping and torturing her?

Because I'm not heartless.

Lorenzo sat in the chair across from me and went back to eating his steak as if no time had passed. He drank from his wineglass, his deep brown irises aimed at me. I took that as my cue to shove the steak into my mouth.

Back in high school, I thought Luca was the cruelest man alive. But the Mafia Don scared the fucking shit out of me.

He instilled the fear of the Devil.

I doubted he ever heard the word no.

My mother would suffer a fate worse than death. She deserved it. Her actions had earned her a special place in Hell.

Lorenzo wiped his mouth with the cloth napkin and tossed it onto the table. I felt his eyes on me before I looked at him.

With the knife in my hand under the table, I braced myself for a fight. I wasn't stupid enough to think Lorenzo would treat me any better than my mother. This lunch was a peace offering to keep me compliant until the wedding that would never fucking happen.

Lorenzo finished his meal a few minutes later, then got up from his chair. "Take your time," he said in a deep tone that rolled down my spine. "Finish your meal. My men will escort you to your room."

I swallowed the lump forming at the back of my throat. "What about my brother?"

His dark eyebrows rose. "What about him?"

"I'd like Aiden to accompany me."

Lorenzo shoved his hands into his pockets, pushing his suit jacket to the side. "He tried to fight my men."

My eyes immediately went to the guns holstered on his chest and then back to his face. "My brother will be on his best behavior from now on. Promise."

"He's a Knight," he said as if that explained everything.

"Not yet. He hasn't finished initiation."

"Doesn't matter," he growled. "The Knights have brainwashed your brother. He's trained to kill. I can't trust him not to act out again."

He bent down on one knee and took my hand. His sudden movement surprised me.

"Lorenzo," I whispered, unable to keep my voice calm and level. "Please don't hurt my brother. He's the only family I have left."

He raised my hand to his mouth and kissed my skin. "You will be my wife seven hours from now." His soft lips brushed my knuckles. "I am your family now." He moved his hand to my stomach. "We will raise this child together."

How did he know?

Apart from the family doctor and now Aiden, no one other than my men knew about the baby. Since we didn't know the paternity of the child, we wanted to keep it a secret until we could determine which of them fathered the baby.

Did Lorenzo spy on us in the room downstairs? Had he overheard my conversation with Aiden?

Talking back to Lorenzo would end with a punishment. I had a child to think about now. Mothers had to protect their babies, so I pressed my lips together and nodded.

Lorenzo reached into his pocket and produced a small velvet box. He cracked open the top and slipped a massive diamond ring on my finger.

Lorenzo kissed the top of my hand one more time, and then he glanced over his shoulder at his men. "Take my bride to her room after she's eaten. She needs her rest."

He didn't look back as he left the room. The moment he was gone, I let out a breath of air, barely able to contain my tears as the first one slid down my cheek.

Chapter Seven

ALEX

After lunch, Lorenzo's men locked me in a private bedroom with an ensuite bathroom. I hopped into the shower and scrubbed my skin until I felt less dirty.

The second I got into the room, I ripped off his stupid engagement ring and replaced it with my real one. I would have rather died than marry Lorenzo Basile. There was no fucking way in hell I could go through with the wedding, not when I was madly in love with my guys.

I tamed my curls with gel and even attempted to do my makeup. It wasn't something I wore often. Growing up, my mother never taught me anything. Aiden showed me how to shave my legs, which was fucking embarrassing. He also watched YouTube videos to help fix my hair so I didn't look like a frizzy rat.

I needed my brother.

He was downstairs in that room alone, and I prayed he was still alive. They didn't have to drag him into this mess.

Lorenzo didn't need to kidnap him.

With a towel wrapped around me, I walked into the bedroom. I flipped the lid off the box, which sat on the king-size mattress. A present from Lorenzo. I rolled my eyes at the white sundress, paired with matching lace panties and a nearly see-through bra.

I dressed into the clothes, since I had nothing else to wear, and then strolled over to the window. Shoving the curtains aside, I looked out at the ocean. Beautiful, peaceful. It would have been perfect if my men were at my sides.

From a distance, I could see land and released a sigh of relief. I couldn't fight him while we were at sea. So I stared out the window and dreamed about how I could kill Lorenzo Basile.

W hat felt like hours passed in silence before one of Lorenzo's men opened the door and dragged me off the boat. We arrived at a small island that could have been anywhere in the world. There was nothing but ocean for miles in every direction.

A jungle surrounded the island. As we walked inland, I saw the mansion guarded by armed men. A tall iron fence, which circled the property, had at least a dozen more security guards lining the perimeter. My men would not get anywhere near this place without getting shot.

A chill rushed down my spine at the thought. They would risk their lives for me. The Devil's Knights had sworn an oath to protect their queen. I didn't want anyone to die for me. My life wasn't any more important than theirs, yet I knew they would take risks, despite the cost.

Several men stood in front of the entrance. They had machine guns strapped to their backs and handguns holstered beneath their suit jackets. Devil Island had more security than a military base.

Lorenzo rushed past us, muttering a few words to the

guards in Italian. He walked through the gates without glancing at me, and I was thankful for that.

I hadn't seen my brother or mother in hours. Aiden was unconscious the last time I saw him. And who knew what the hell those men had done to my mother?

The men gripping my arms led me through the gates and into a massive courtyard with even more guards. The salty scent of the ocean floated through the air like perfume. This was a fortress on the sea, similar to the Salvatore Estate.

My home.

An ache spread through my chest when I thought about Luca, Marcello, Damian, and Bastian. I dreamed of the moment I could throw myself into their arms.

I stared at the back of Lorenzo as he blew past the guards, moving through the courtyard with speed. He was in his fifties and attractive for a man his age. In some ways, he reminded me of Arlo Salvatore. Refined, polished, like he thought he was better than everyone else. With one look, you could tell he had money, and judging by his yacht and this island, he had tons of it.

He dashed through the courtyard, dressed in white linen shorts, a button-down shirt, and boat shoes. His naturally olive skin popped against the light clothing.

We followed Lorenzo into the house and stepped into the Tuscan-style foyer. The ceiling was high, the walls various shades of cream and decorated with fine art. It didn't look like somewhere you would hold a secret auction for the world's criminals.

I recognized the paintings on the walls as we moved down a long tiled hallway. More Evangeline Franco pieces. My fingers itched to be back in Evangeline's studio, creating more paintings in the Many Faces of the Devil series. I wanted so badly to be back home with my handsome princes, so I could start my life with them.

The men forced me upstairs, with one in front of me and

the other man grabbing my ass to push me up each step. I swatted his hand and yelled.

When we reached the top of the landing, Lorenzo waited for us in the hallway. "Take your hands off my fiancée before I break them."

"Sorry, sir." He lowered his head. "It won't happen again."

"You wouldn't touch the paintings on my walls," he snapped in a cold tone that crawled down my arms. "So why did you think you could touch my woman?"

I wanted to correct him, but I knew I had to play the game. Let him think I belonged to him.

"Take Alexandrea to her room," Lorenzo ordered. "Send the seamstress upstairs for the dress fitting."

His eyes landed on my face, then moved to my breasts for a second before he looked at me again. I wanted to cut out his black heart and shove it down his throat.

I glared at him, hating the feeling of his eyes on my skin. He opened his mouth as if he were about to speak, and then he took off down the hallway without another word.

A fter Lorenzo left us, a man with short, dark hair and scruff along his jaw pushed me into a large bedroom with his hand on my back. He forced me to sit in front of a vanity, where a pretty brunette waited for me with a makeup brush in her hand.

She didn't even look at me as she worked on my face. Another woman gathered my curls in her hand and pinned them into an updo. I sat in complete silence as they treated me like a doll.

After my hair and makeup were complete, I looked in the

mirror. I didn't recognize the woman who stared back at me. Charcoal eye shadow lined my eyes, paired with a sultry blue. My lips looked plump and fuller than usual from the pink gloss.

The brunette woman lifted a white gown from a hanger and held it for me. My throat closed up at the sight of my wedding dress. It had a sexy corset top that would show way too much cleavage. The fabric was lacy and had a long train that seemed endless.

Other women would have drooled over this gown. But as I gazed at it, tears pricked my eyes.

I wanted to scream.

The girl took the dress off the hanger and held it out for me to step into it.

I bit my lip and shook my head.

"If you don't put this on, Mr. Basile will shove you into it and drag you down the aisle. It's the easy way or the hard way."

"I don't want to marry him," I muttered.

"You don't have a choice," she snapped. "No one tells Mr. Basile no." She moved closer to me, the dress fisted in her hands. "Put on the dress, and you can see your brother before the ceremony."

I hopped up from the bench and stepped into the dress. Maybe Aiden would have some ideas about getting us out of this situation.

She pulled the gown up my body and zipped it behind me. When I gazed into the mirror, my heart dropped into my stomach. I looked like any other bride on her wedding day.

This felt wrong.

Disgusting.

I clutched my stomach, bending forward to quell the rising sickness at the back of my throat. She steered me over to the vanity by my shoulder and pushed me onto the bench.

"Just breathe," she lilted. "It will be over soon."

Holding my hand over my heart, I breathed, reminding myself it would all work out in the end.

A few minutes later, the door opened.

Aiden walked into the room, dressed in a black tuxedo, his wayward blond curls gelled to keep them off his forehead. He looked handsome with his face shaved. Without the facial hair, the dimple in his right cheek popped when he forced a smile for my benefit.

I extended my hand to him. "Aiden."

He crossed the room, took my hand, and got on one knee in front of me. A few errant tears slid down my cheeks, messing up the makeup caked on my face. My brother wiped them away with his fingers.

"You look beautiful, Lexie." He pulled me into his arms and whispered, "I will get you out of here."

"How?" I asked in a hushed tone. "They have guards everywhere."

"The Salvatores are here with some of the Knights. I over-heard Lorenzo telling the guards to keep their eyes on them. He knows they're going to stop the wedding."

I glanced over at the girl who helped me into my dress. She leaned against the doorframe and flirted with a guard.

We had little time to talk, so I leaned into my twin and lowered my voice. "They're going to get themselves killed."

"They wouldn't come here without a plan," he assured me.

"Have you seen them? Are they armed?"

He shook his head. "They don't allow weapons on the island."

I blew out a deep breath, my heart racing in my chest. Unfortunately, this conversation didn't bring me any comfort.

"Luca is one of the craziest people I have ever met," Aiden said. "But he's also the smartest. He wouldn't come here without an exit strategy."

I chuckled. "That must have killed you to say that."

He smirked. "Luca is a lot of things. But he's not an idiot." Aiden squeezed my hand to comfort me. "I will do everything I can to stop you from marrying Lorenzo. So will the Salvatore brothers and the Knights. We took an oath, Lexie. Protect our queen at all costs." His hand moved to the back of my head and kissed my forehead. "Even if I hadn't made the oath before the Knights, I will always put your life before mine."

A cell phone rang in the hallway, snapping my attention back to the guards.

One of them entered the room and raised his hand. "Let's go!"

I glanced at Aiden.

"It's okay, Lexie." He rubbed my shoulders. "I'm right here."

Chapter Eight

LUCA

We boarded a private jet at an airstrip in Hartford and headed toward Florida with the Knights. From Key West, we would charter a boat to the island where they were holding the Il Circo auction.

I finished the rest of my scotch, set the glass on the table, and pushed myself up from the chair. Marcello looked in my direction. I gestured for him to follow me into the back of the plane, away from the Knights. He hadn't spoken a word since we received the invitation to the island.

We entered the bedroom.

Marcello shut the door. I sat on the bed and leaned forward, resting my elbows on my thighs.

"We'll find her." My brother dropped to the bed beside me. "Our plan will work. Trust me."

Scrubbing a hand across my jaw, I sighed. "We need to prepare ourselves for the possibility…"

I couldn't even finish my thought.

"Lorenzo needs Alex," he said with certainty in his tone. "He won't hurt her."

"But he's unpredictable. He can turn on the charm and

make you think he's your best friend. And the next second, he stabs you in the back. I bet he's giving Alex the royal treatment, making her believe he's not a bad guy. That he doesn't want to hurt her."

"I'm afraid for Alex." He aimed his sad blue eyes at me. "What concerns me most is the mental torture she's enduring right now. This is too much for someone with her illness. She may never recover."

"Alex is tougher than you think," I shot back. "Give her some credit, Marcello. She put up with all of our shit for years. Our girl isn't a delicate flower anymore."

Marcello shook his head. "Alex has been through hell, but nothing like this. We may need to hospitalize her after we get her back. She was already fragile before the kidnapping."

"Alex is family." I squeezed his shoulder. "And we protect our family. So we'll do whatever is necessary to help her."

He nodded. "Anything for our queen."

I gave him a surprising one-arm hug. At first, Marcello tensed because this was an unusual exchange for us. But then he pulled me into his arms like he needed this hug.

We were both scared of what our enemies would do to her. Physical pain was nothing compared to emotional pain. This was the reason I didn't allow myself to feel. The reason I never wanted to let Alex into my heart.

Losing her broke me.

It broke all four of us.

Marcello cupped my shoulder, then got up from the bed. "I have to speak with my team before we land."

Before we left Devil's Creek, Marcello devised a multi-step plan with Alpha Command. There was no way for the Knights to attack the island head-on. They would likely force us to check our weapons at the door. All of our names were on the list, placed our bids to get onto the island.

Alpha Command divers would swim to the island, armed

and ready to take out the guards. It was the only shot we had of getting Alex away from Lorenzo. Of course, he wouldn't see it coming. Not with us playing the game, acting like willing participants at the auction.

"Our divers will enter through the jungle," Marcello said in a firm tone. "There's less security on the north side of the island."

"Lorenzo won't do anything to Alex until he's off the island. So we have that working in our favor."

He tapped my back. "I fucked up before with The Mansion, the attack at the house, and Alex's kidnapping. But this time, I have a solid plan. I've worked out every detail with my men. Do you trust me?"

I held his gaze for a moment and nodded.

O nce we landed in Key West, we boarded a boat and headed toward an island between the Florida Keys and the Dry Tortugas. As we sped toward the island, The Knights gathered around me on leather couches in the saloon. I ran our plan past the Knights, detailing each of Marcello's backup plans in case we had to change course.

Everyone was on board with the dual-prong attack on the island. Marcello's men would eliminate the guards, working their way around the perimeter until we had control.

"We'll only get one shot at taking Alex off the island," Sonny said, his voice rougher than usual.

None of us had slept much in the past twenty-four hours. The adrenaline coursing through my veins kept me awake. I couldn't relax until I had Alex in my arms.

Not long ago, I wanted her to suffer for her mother's

actions. But she worked her voodoo on my brothers and me, casting all four of us under her spell.

"The Luciano brothers are our best chance of extracting Alex from the island," I told them. "I spoke with Dante before we left the port. My cousins are on standby until they hear from us."

Drake sneered. "So we're supposed to sit at the auction, drink scotch, and pretend like those assholes didn't steal our queen?"

I held up my hand to silence him. "We follow the plan. Act like nothing is wrong."

"Lorenzo isn't stupid," Sonny shot back. "He knows we're coming for her. This is a fool's mission to walk in there as if we're bidding on the auction."

I gritted my teeth. "You don't think I know this, Cormac? Keep your ears and eyes open." My gaze drifted to each of the Knights. "Look for anything out of the ordinary."

"We're going to a private auction for the world's richest deviants," Hunter Banks said with laughter in his tone. "What exactly counts as ordinary?"

Drake slid a hand through his dark hair and laughed. "He has a point."

I waved my hand to dismiss him. "We're at a disadvantage on the island. Accept it. This is the risk we must take to get back our queen."

Sonny chugged the contents of his glass and slammed it down on the table. "Anyone up for a gentleman's wager?"

Bastian leaned forward on the couch, a sly grin on his face as he looked at Sonny. "What do you have in mind?"

My brother loved a good bet.

"Ten thousand says we won't make it past security with our weapons."

Drake smirked. "I'll take that bet."

I moved between them and threw out my hands. "This is

not the time for games. Alex's life is on the line. All of our lives are at stake."

"Chill." Bastian pushed out his palm. "Let us do our thing before we go to war."

"Taking bets on us losing the war is not fucking funny!"

"I said they wouldn't let us bring our guns," Sonny commented. "Just stating a fact, Salvatore. Marcello and his team have already accounted for that variable."

I pushed my hands to my hips, my gaze traveling between them. "We dock in twenty minutes. Get your heads back in the game."

W e arrived at *Isola del Diavolo*, also known as Devil Island. Dock lights illuminated the palm trees. Through the thick encasement, I could see a glimpse of the seaside fortress that looked like it could withstand any attack.

As we walked through the forest, men guided us down a lit path toward the gate surrounding the Tuscan-style mansion. From the look of it, they had more security on this side of the island, which made sense.

Drake Battle's artificial intelligence software helped us gain some insight into the layout of the island, down to the number of guards posted at each end of the property. We knew the guards' shifts and even identified a few. They were Sicilian, Made men tied to the Calabrian crime family.

I shoved my cell phone into the inner pocket of my suit jacket as we stopped at the gate. A dark-haired man around the same height as me ran his hands over my back, shoulders, and chest, all the way down my arms and legs. I handed over my guns before he continued his slow exploration.

The Knights followed suit.

Marcello moved to my right as Damian and Bastian clung to my left side. We walked through the gates and into the busy courtyard as a team. I recognized a few men we'd given loans for their shady businesses. They nodded while others glared at us.

At this place, we had just as many allies as enemies. It was impossible to know who was working with the Basile crime family.

Men smoked cigars and sipped from snifters as we passed them. Before we reached the front doors of the estate, a man I recognized strolled through them.

Lorenzo Basile.

I thought about his stupid fucking note in the shipping container and wanted to spit in his face. It wasn't just a message to my family. His note was a lesson not to fuck with the Sicilian Mafia.

"Luca." Lorenzo extended his hand. "Welcome to my home." His gaze drifted to each of my brothers and then to the Knights. "Gentleman."

People in our world claimed The Lucaya Group ran Il Circo, but the group's leaders were a mystery. No one, not even the CIA, had enough intelligence on the terrorist organization. We assumed the Russians were behind it because an ex-KGB officer posed as the head of the organization. But he was a ghost, untouchable, and therefore the perfect scapegoat.

The Russians were the tip of the iceberg. They never wanted Alex. It was always about Viktor Romanov's daughter for them. But for the man standing before me, this was about revenge.

Payback for my mother.

He had the one thing all of us valued most in his possession.

Our queen.

No money or favors could ever satisfy his need to avenge my mother's death.

Lorenzo placed his hand on my shoulder with a sick grin pulling at his mouth. "The auction is about to start. Glad you could join us."

I met his cold, hard stare, pretending as if he hadn't gotten under my skin. "I wouldn't miss it."

Chapter Nine

ALEX

With a face full of makeup and wearing a wedding dress given to me by another man, I walked down the spiral staircase with my brother. My throat was about to close up from the nerves choking me. Between my raging anxiety and my waves of pregnancy sickness, I struggled to keep down the food in my stomach.

The estate was massive, with high ceilings, ornate molding, and marble floors that glistened when the fluorescent lights hit them. It reminded me of the Salvatore Estate, from the expensive paintings which donned the walls to the sixteenth-century Italian architecture which filled every room.

Aiden clutched my hand, holding me close to his side. Like he was afraid if he let go, I would drift away. After months of separation, I was happy to have him by my side. But not under these circumstances.

I was already engaged to four other men, one of which had put his child inside me. My chest ached when I thought about them. About how this would crush each of them in different ways. There was no way they would get me off this island, not without getting themselves killed.

Guards surrounded the place like it was a military base on the sea. The only way off the island was by boat. You could hear and see everyone coming and going from the island. So unless my men stole a submarine, we were stuck here, entirely at the mercy of the terrifying Mafia boss.

I tried to stay positive and believe in a happily ever after with my guys. But I also understood the odds. They would die trying to get me off this island. And they would all do it willingly because I was their queen. Because love was a powerful weapon that could lighten even the darkest heart.

When my feet hit the ground floor, a wave of nausea swept over me, rocking me to the core. I dug my fingers into Aiden's arm to steady myself.

He lowered his head, eyes on me. "Are you okay?"

"I've been sick for weeks."

A guard tapped my back with his hand and pushed me forward. "Keep moving."

We walked down a long tiled hallway guarded by men dressed in suits, armed and dangerous. They had stoic expressions plastered on their faces. None of them looked directly at us, but I could still feel their eyes on me.

Our entourage surrounded us—two men at the front, two in the back, and two on each side. Aiden was crazy to think he could get me out of here.

We had zero chance.

The guards steered us into a massive ballroom. It had tall windows and a high ceiling with a gorgeous crystal chandelier hanging in the center. The space was large enough to host a wedding. Round tables and chairs separated the aisle that led to a platform with a podium for the auctioneer.

As we walked past the first few tables, heads snapped in my direction. Men with dark tattoos, gnarly scars, and scary gazes stared back at me. They looked like men hardened by their work—criminals dressed in suits to make them look more legitimate.

My breath caught in my throat when I spotted Luca, Marcello, Bastian, and Damian on the opposite side of the room. They stood beside Lorenzo, who had his hand on Luca's shoulder, drinking amber liquid from a highball glass as if they were old friends.

Strange men licked their lips as I passed their tables. I was already a D cup before the baby hormones, and now that my boobs were getting bigger, this dress barely contained them. I felt so vulnerable and exposed, on display for some of the sickest men in the world.

Lorenzo tapped Luca on the shoulder, then turned his attention to me. As his gaze met mine, Luca's lips parted. His eyes traveled up and down the length of the wedding gown.

I had the attention of all my men.

Marcello's sad blue eyes held mine captive as he shook his head. He hated seeing me in another man's dress. Damian looked as if he had gone to his dark mental place. I hoped he would keep his cool long enough to get out of here.

I left Bastian for last, finding it unbearable to let him see me like this. Teeth clenched, he balled his hands into fists at his sides. I watched his chest rise and fall, his breathing growing more erratic as he studied every inch of my body.

None of them could make any sudden movements or show Lorenzo they cared. They had to pretend I was nothing more than a plaything. A way for their family to get revenge for their mother's murder.

It was what I would have done.

I would have made it look like they were my enemy. That was the only way they would survive this nightmare.

For years, they had shut off their emotions. They tuned out the world and pretended they didn't care about anything. I had to remind myself of that when Luca turned away from me. He said something to Lorenzo and rolled his shoulders.

The guards halted when we reached the end of the long

carpeted aisle. Lorenzo stepped away from my guys with an evil grin in place.

His thumb brushed my cheek, his skin rough against mine. "You're a beautiful bride, Alexandrea."

He set off down the aisle alone, leaving me standing there without further instruction. I figured it wouldn't be a traditional wedding. No bridal music or bridesmaids. But it surprised me when Lorenzo stood beside a priest on the platform.

Aiden extended his hand to me and whispered, "You can do this."

I glanced over at my guys, begging them with my eyes to do something. Marcello gave me a reassuring nod. That was all I needed to take Aiden's hand.

Sweat coated my palm, forcing my brother to tighten his grip as he led me down the aisle. I felt like I was walking down a plank to my death. Like I was two seconds from falling off the edge of a boat, about to drown in a sea of nothingness.

At least Aiden was with me.

My guys were here, too.

Lorenzo grabbed the microphone from the podium. "Thank you for joining us on *Isola del Diavolo*. Your bids have secured you a seat at the table. But the real fun will start after I take care of important business." He pulled me closer. "Do you see this beautiful woman? Her name is Alexandrea Wellington."

An echo of gasps went around the room. A few of the men even clapped.

"She's the only living granddaughter of Carl Wellington. I know most of you are familiar with our history. But for those unaware, fifteen years ago, Alexandrea's mother murdered my beloved niece, Evangeline. She took her from my family. From her sons." He pointed his finger at Luca and Marcello. "Their father covered up her death with a car accident. My nephews colluded with the Wellingtons." A grin tipped up the corners of his mouth. "I have long waited to repay the Wellingtons and the Salvatores for their sins."

Out of the corner of my eye, I spotted a man dragging a woman onto the stage with us. My mouth dropped at the sight of my mother held at gunpoint. Covered in black and blue bruises from head to toe, she limped as the man shoved her toward Lorenzo.

I almost felt bad for her.

Almost.

As I thought about the hell she put me through as a child, any sympathy I felt for her disappeared. Years of locked rooms and closets. My screams for help. Eighteen long years of torture until my grandfather saved us.

Lorenzo wrapped his hands around my mother's throat. A sick part of me enjoyed it. I liked seeing her weak and at the mercy of a monster.

My eyes flicked over to my men, where guards surrounded them. On the opposite side of the room, I found Drake, Sonny, and his brothers accompanied by a few Knights I hadn't seen before.

I turned to face Lorenzo, who closed his fingers over my mother's throat so hard she gasped for air. He tossed her at a guard like she was a piece of trash. The man pointed a gun at her head, and she begged him to let her go.

Laughter filled the silence in the room. Everyone in the crowd watched as the scene played out before them like a fucked up movie.

Lorenzo took his place beside the priest.

The priest looked at my brother and said, "Who gives this woman to marry this man?"

Aiden swallowed hard as he looked at me. Biting the inside of my cheek, I nodded.

He had to do this.

We were out-manned, outgunned, and disadvantaged on the island. The wedding didn't mean shit. It probably wasn't even legal. Lorenzo could force my hand, but he would never have me.

"I do," Aiden bit out.

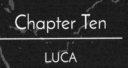

Chapter Ten

LUCA

I couldn't breathe as I looked at her. Dressed in a white wedding gown that fit her curves perfectly, Alex looked like a fucking goddess.

Like a queen.

Our girl was perfection in every way. The one good thing all four of us had in our lives. Without her, we wouldn't survive. She had her hooks in all of us, holding our black hearts in her hand with the power to crush them.

Losing her would kill us.

She stood beside Lorenzo in front of the priest, shifting her weight nervously from one foot to the other. Her eyes drifted over her shoulder at us. She was waiting for us to step in and save the day.

But none of us could move.

Not even an inch.

Several men surrounded us on each side, armed. Of course, we knew going into this situation we wouldn't have access to a weapon. But, despite our apparent disadvantages on the island, we weren't out of options. Lorenzo and his men didn't know we had Alpha Command working quietly outside these walls to disarm the guards.

Lorenzo tugged on Alex's hand, snapping her attention back to the priest. They went through the motions of a typical wedding. Lorenzo was Catholic and wanted a proper wedding spoken in Italian. This bought us some time.

I turned my head to look at Marcello, who signaled Alpha Command would arrive in five minutes. With that, my racing heart slowed to a more normal rate.

A sudden calm washed over me.

My father had shown us from an early age that weaknesses would get us killed. That our enemies would sniff them out and use them against us. Back then, I never thought a woman could be a weakness. I hadn't known that falling in love with a woman could destroy me.

I.

Fucking.

Loved.

Her.

She had begged for my love and affection. But it wasn't until she learned the truth about our families that I felt the burden lift off my shoulders. Over the past few months, Alex had shown me that love was more than words. It was actions, devotion, and this sickening feeling I got when I thought about someone hurting her.

Marcello tapped my arm with his elbow. I glanced over at him, and he nodded to signal we had one minute to go. We needed to prepare Aiden, if possible. He was on Alex's left side, his eyes moving between Alex and us.

I raised my arm a few inches and pointed at my watch, holding up one finger.

His head barely moved, but I knew he understood what I was trying to tell him. Aiden was artsy and a free spirit like his sister, but he wasn't an idiot. He knew what was at stake for all of us.

One of Lorenzo's men curled his arm around Alex's

mother, and a gun pressed to her head. She squirmed in his arms, even though it was pointless.

She deserved to die for her sins.

A loud bang at the back of the ballroom ended the ceremony. The windows exploded on impact, glass shattering across the room. Gunshots rang out, one after the other. Lorenzo's guards attempted to shoot as dozens of men from Alpha Command swarmed the room, dressed in full gear.

Several men threw flash-bang canisters. People started coughing. Some tried to run, but the thick smoke made it hard to see more than a few feet in front of me.

As planned, I dropped to the floor beside my brothers and covered my mouth with my jacket. White smoke from the canisters filled the air. I looked up just in time to see Aiden grab Alex.

Of course, Lorenzo wouldn't go down without a fight. He shot at them, the bullet missing Alex and grazing Aiden's shoulder. A team of men advanced on him. Quick on his feet, Lorenzo grabbed Savanna and ran out of the room in the opposite direction.

As Alex and Aiden snuck out of the ballroom, I sighed. Lorenzo was on the run with Alex's mother, but at least our girl was safe.

Chapter Eleven

ALEX

S hards of glass rained down on the guests, the room filled with a vinegar scent, and white smoke rose from the floor. My heart raced at the sound of several gunshots, one after the other.

I trembled with each shot, my body shaking so badly I was thankful for Aiden when he hooked his arm around me. He steered me away from Lorenzo, who shouted my name over the uproar in the room.

Men dressed in black camouflage invaded the ballroom, shooting at the guards. The guests couldn't bring their weapons into the mansion. That was our only saving grace. Otherwise, this place would have been a bloodbath.

My men dropped to the floor as if on cue. I should have known they wouldn't come to the island without a plan. None of my men were stupid. They always did things with a purpose.

Until a minute ago, I thought I would have to marry Lorenzo to get out of here alive. All so my guys wouldn't have to leave the island in body bags.

Aiden lifted me off the platform and dragged me toward the hallway, ordering me to cover my mouth and nose with my hand. A bullet whizzed past my ear and hit my brother in the shoulder.

"Aiden!" I shouted, tears stinging my eyes.

He winced in pain, but he didn't let the wound or the blood seeping through his shirt deter him. "I'm okay," he bit out. "Let's go."

Aiden guided me toward the first door on our right. Inside, the room was pitch black, with only a sliver of moonlight, which cast a shadow on the hardwood floor.

He locked the door behind us and placed his hands on my shoulders. "Lexie, listen to me. I know you hate the dark, but we can't turn on the lights."

I swallowed the lump at the back of my throat. "Tell me what to do."

He led me toward the windows and shoved the curtains aside. Aiden got on the windowsill and pushed out the casement windows as far as they would go. Then he lifted me and set me on the ledge. "Jump. You can do this, Lexie." He rubbed his palm on my back. "Jump. I'll be right behind you."

I was terrified, but I trusted my brother and his instincts, so I jumped out the window. Aiden hopped down a second later, and we ran across the lawn.

My brother clutched my hand as we hauled ass into the jungle. I swatted at low-hanging branches, ignoring the random animal noises that slithered down my spine. Fueled by fear and adrenaline, I moved as fast as my feet would allow in a pair of heels. It wasn't easy running through mud and dirt. A few times, my heels got stuck, and Aiden had to pull me out.

Once we reached the dock, we stopped to look at several boats anchored to the shore. But the dark-haired man dressed in a suit stole my attention. He stood on the dock beside a yacht with his hands stuffed into the pockets of his slacks.

I recognized the tall and imposing man from the party at the Salvatore Estate. Dante Luciano was the head of a crime family in Atlantic City. He was Luca and Marcello's cousin on their mother's side and related to Lorenzo Basile.

Aiden moved toward him.

I yanked on his hand, forcing him to stop. "We can't trust him."

"Dante is cool," he shot back. "He'll get us out of here."

I shook my head. "For all we know, he was part of Lorenzo's plan."

Even though we spoke in hushed tones, Dante must have heard us. He inched toward us, his hands raised in the air. "I'm not here to hurt you, Alexandrea. Luca called me. I'm your ride home."

I pushed out my palm to stop him. "What about Luca and his brothers?"

"They'll join us soon," he said.

I wrapped my arms around my middle to steady the nerves coursing through my veins. "I'm not leaving here without them."

Aiden shook my shoulder, but his voice sounded far away. "Hey, Lexie, look at me."

I blinked a few times as I looked up at my brother, who towered over me. Physically, I stood before him, but I felt like my body was somewhere else. Somewhere far, far away from the island.

"We don't have time for this," Dante snapped.

He removed a cell phone from his pocket, dialed a number, and put it on speakerphone. It rang a few times before I heard Luca's voice.

Luca.

His deep voice snapped me back to reality for a moment.

"I have your queen," Dante said with his eyes on me. "But she won't leave with me."

"Drea," Luca choked out, his breathing labored as if he were running. "Listen to me, baby. Go with Dante. We'll see you soon."

As if my body was performing the motions without my brain fully understanding, I closed the distance between us and took the phone from Dante's hand. "Luca, are you okay?"

"Yeah, baby." He breathed into the receiver. "We're fine. Just get on the boat with Dante."

His words said one thing, but his tone said another. He sounded anything but fine.

"Okay." I bit my lip. "All four of you better return to me in one piece."

He groaned.

Then the line went dead.

Chapter Twelve

LUCA

A lex was on the Luciano brothers' boat, headed back to Key West. My cousins wanted Lorenzo removed from power. So I offered the Knights' support and our resources for their help.

With the island under our control, we walked around the place like fucking kings. Men tipped their heads at us. Some even asked for our assistance with their illegal businesses. Not like we had time to talk shop with these idiots. They could wait until we were home.

"Lorenzo is gone," Marcello told me. "I spoke with my team leader, and they can't find him or Savanna."

"Fuck," I grunted.

Bastian moved beside me as we walked across the lawn and into the jungle. "The highest bid on Alex was thirty million dollars. We got her back, but there's still a bounty on her head."

"Whoever listed her for sale produced her tonight. Technically, they satisfied their part of the deal."

"But we don't know who won her," Bastian pointed out. "Which means we don't know who will come for her."

"My guess would be Lorenzo. He orchestrated the event to get us to the island."

Bastian nodded. "But what if it wasn't him?"

"After tonight, it doesn't matter. Lorenzo's men conspired with us. They want him dead even more than we do."

We boarded a seaplane that had just enough room to fit a few of the Knights. Marcello sat beside me on the plane with his hand on my knee. He was better at communicating his feelings.

Alex had shown me I didn't have to be a corpse all the time. So I grabbed my brother's hand.

Twenty minutes later, we landed the plane in the water beside the Luciano brother's yacht. Two men leaned overboard and threw ropes at us. I grabbed one rope, and Marcello took the other.

Slow and steady, we climbed up the side of the boat. More athletic and conditioned for battle, Marcello was already on board, lending a helping hand when my feet hit the deck.

"You're out of shape." Marcello slapped me on the back and laughed. "You should come for a run with me when we get back to Devil's Creek."

I rolled my eyes at him. "I work out seven days a week. I'm good."

Damian and Bastian climbed up the ropes behind us. I waved to Drake, Sonny, Callum, and Finn.

A dark-haired man raised his hand, then turned his back to us. "Dante is waiting for you."

The seaplane floated across the Atlantic Ocean, eventually lifting into the air. I followed Dante's right-hand man into the cabin. We walked down a long hallway that had a Tuscan-style vibe that reminded me of Dante's casino.

He had inherited The Portofino Hotel and Casino in Atlantic City after a rival family murdered his father last year. It was one of many legitimate businesses his family used to launder drug money.

We entered the last room on the right.

Dante sat behind a long mahogany desk with his younger brothers, Stefan and Angelo, in the chairs across from him. Even Nicodemus, the black sheep of the family, was in attendance. All four of them rose from their chairs as we entered the room.

Dante moved out from behind the desk with a proud grin. "You made it."

I shook his hand. "Thanks to you." We embraced for a second, and then our eyes met. "Where is Alex?"

He tipped his head toward the couch. "She passed out the second her head hit the pillow."

"Where's Aiden?"

"He's getting stitched up," Dante confirmed. "He took a bullet to the shoulder on his way out of the mansion."

I narrowed my eyes at him. "A flesh wound?"

He nodded.

After almost losing Marcello, our girl couldn't handle another shooting. Alex would fall apart without her twin brother.

She slept soundly on a plush couch, her head propped up on a stack of pillows. Someone had covered her with a blanket. I wanted to rip the fucking wedding dress off her beautiful body and shred it to pieces.

I approached the couch with Dante at my side. "Did she say anything before she fell asleep?"

He shook his head. "Not much. She kept talking about a dark closet and mumbled something to Aiden about their mother."

"Fuck." I raked a hand through my hair and groaned. "Did she seem like she wasn't with the program?"

"Yeah, I guess." He shrugged. "Aiden told us about her condition. So we gave her a sedative to calm her down."

I dropped to my knees beside the couch, studying her face.

Then, brushing Alex's hair off her forehead, I pressed my lips to her skin.

No matter what condition, I would always want her. She was my girl from the moment I laid eyes on her. So beautiful and pure, I had dreamed of all the ways I would break her. But I never anticipated that she would change me. I never expected her to make me feel again.

"Drea," I whispered into her ear. "Wake up, baby girl."

Marcello dropped to his knees on my right, Damian and Bastian on my left. I stroked her cheek with my knuckles, and she stirred from my touch. She rolled onto her side and curled up into a ball. Her chest rose and fell.

"You're safe now," I whispered. "We won't let anyone touch you ever again."

Marcello clutched her hand. "We're here, princess."

She looked up at me, her eyes bloodshot and watery. Her gaze flicked to each of my brothers, and she took a relieved breath. "You're alive. Thank God." Alex covered her heart with her hand. "Where's Aiden?"

"He's fine," Marcello assured her, making a slow, circular motion on top of her hand to ease her concern.

"Someone shot him," she whimpered.

I slid my fingers down her arm to soothe her. "Dante's men stitched him up, gave him some pain meds. He's taking a nap."

Alex blew out a deep breath. "How did you make it off the island alive?"

Marcello smirked. "You should know by now we always have a plan."

Her stomach growled.

I shoved the blanket off her to touch her belly and feel the slight baby bump. It wasn't noticeable, but I knew every curve of her body. "When was the last time you ate?"

"On Lorenzo's boat," she muttered with one eye open. "But I couldn't keep the food down."

"You need to eat something," Bastian said before I could get out the words.

Damian leaned over her and extended his hand. "Sit up, Pet."

With his help, she propped herself up. "I was afraid I wouldn't see any of you again. I missed you guys."

Bastian patted her knee. "We missed you, too, Cherry."

I clutched her shoulder.

She groaned as if my touch branded her skin.

"Are you hurt?"

Alex shook her head, blonde curls falling in front of her eyes. "No, not really. I feel like shit from being drugged and thrown around by my kidnappers."

I slid my fingers beneath her chin to steal her gaze back to me. "Did Lorenzo touch you?"

"No. He wouldn't even let his men touch me."

"When we get home, you're seeing a doctor." I rubbed my palm over her stomach. "The drugs could have hurt the baby."

She placed her hand over mine, a grin plastered on her gorgeous face. "I love how protective you are over her."

"Her?" My eyebrows rose an inch. "You don't know it's a girl."

"Call it a gut feeling." She moved our hands over the top of the dress in a circular motion. "Would that upset you?"

I shook my head.

"I'd love to have a little girl," Marcello interjected.

She smiled at him. "You'd be a good girl-dad."

"What about me?" Bastian asked.

She stretched out her fingers to touch his hand. "I think you'll be a great dad, Bash."

Damian didn't speak, barely even breathed, as Alex looked at him. He was terrified of having a child and never considered being a father.

"You too, Damian," she muttered. "Once you overcome your fear, it will come naturally to you."

I knew we'd have kids because of the deal with The Founders Society. But my anxiety over having a child running around the mansion didn't compare to Damian's.

One of Dante's men appeared behind me with plates of food for Alex. He set the dishes beside me and walked out of the room without a word.

"You need to eat." I fisted the burger and held it in front of her mouth. "Open up, Drea."

She licked her lips and bit into the burger like a good girl.

Chapter Thirteen

ALEX

It was all a dream. That was what I told myself repeatedly, hoping I would believe the lie. After the events of the past two days, I was numb. Dead on the inside, trapped inside an alternate version of reality.

I stared at the wall as Pops examined my face. Something had snapped inside me after I got onto the Lucianos yacht and saw the blood soaking through Aiden's jacket and shirt.

Lorenzo shot him.

My mind drifted back to the dark closet and the feeling of the walls closing in on me. The never-ending silence. Then my screams, Aiden banging on the wall. My mother's laughter.

She kidnapped me.

As if she hadn't already done enough damage to my life, she had to sell me to a man who wanted revenge. At least she got what was coming to her. He would make sure she suffered at his hands.

"Aiden," I whispered.

Luca waved his hand in front of my face.

"Aiden," I said again.

"What's wrong with her?" Luca asked Pops.

My grandfather's nose scrunched as he swiped a curl off

my forehead. "Alex is in shock. Give her time to readjust to her surroundings."

Luca shoved a hand through his dark hair and tugged at the ends. "Will she go back to normal?"

Pops glared at him. "She's never had a normal life. Not with her parents, and certainly not with you and your brothers."

"You know what I mean," Luca shot back. "Will she return to how she was before the kidnapping?"

My grandfather's eyes narrowed. "Years ago, she slipped into a dissociative state that lasted for three weeks. She thought she was twelve years old and still living with her parents."

"Yeah." Luca sighed. "That was my fault, too."

After the night The Serpents chased me through Beacon Bay, I had nightmares for years.

Pops sneered at him. "You better take care of Alex. Her situation is delicate."

"Of course." Luca blew out a deep breath. "I just…"

"Alex will never be normal. She's gone through too much trauma in her life to bounce back from this as if nothing happened. If Alex's mental illness is too much for you," Pops said in a menacing tone, "maybe you should let her go. Marcello knows how to handle her better than you."

They spoke as if I were not in the room with them. Sure, I was in shock, but I could process their words. Unfortunately, speaking seemed to be a different skill set I didn't possess at the moment.

Did they drug me?

My head felt funny like I was floating above my body but still aware of everything around me. Every time I opened my mouth to speak, nothing came out. I couldn't even form the words to say them aloud.

"If you knew your granddaughter the way I do, you would know she's much stronger than you realize."

71

"I blame you for every bad thing that has happened to her."

"You have every right." Luca stuffed his hands into his pockets. "I will spend the rest of my life regretting my decisions."

Pops gave him a satisfied nod.

Luca squeezed my shoulder like he couldn't believe I was real and had to check.

"Alex needs a bath and some rest," Luca said to Pops. "We can take it from here."

My grandfather removed a bottle of pills from his pocket and handed them to Luca. "See that she takes these until she's feeling better."

Luca glanced at the label on the bottle, then stuffed them into the pocket of his suit jacket.

After Pops left the house, Luca carried me upstairs with his brothers in tow. He sat me on the toilet in the ensuite bathroom in his bedroom. Then, without a word, he got on his knees and filled the massive garden tub with soapy water.

I watched him in action.

When he thought no one was watching him, Luca looked at peace. Like the man he would have become if his mother were still alive.

Marcello kneeled beside me and placed his hand on my thigh. Just the feel of his skin pressed against mine made me feel safe, comforted.

Bastian moved between my spread thighs. He put his head on my stomach and hugged me. "I missed you, Cherry."

I moved my hand to the back of his head and shoved my fingers through his short, brown hair. He lifted his head to look up at me and smiled.

Damian propped himself up against the wall by the window, his intense green eyes on me. I hadn't heard him speak a single word, not even to his brothers.

Was he in shock, too?

"I'm not okay," I whispered.

Luca slipped his fingers between mine. "We know, baby. What I said to your grandfather…" He sighed. "You're not broken. We will get through this together, okay? And we're going to come out of this stronger."

"Thank you," I muttered and meant every word.

"No need to thank me, baby." He cupped my face in his hands and bent down to kiss me. "I'm glad you're home. I know I've been hard on you. I haven't always been the man you deserve. But losing you… It was the worst pain imaginable. I promised myself if I got you back, I would change. I'll be better for you."

"I thought pain is just weakness leaving the body."

"Physical pain, yes." His hands dropped to my thighs. "But I hadn't felt emotional pain since my mom died. It took every ounce of control for me to hold it together."

I stroked his short, black hair with my fingers. It was loose and messy as if he had been pulling on the ends. He usually kept it gelled and spiky. But as our eyes met, he looked more like the damaged boy I'd met years ago.

His thumb brushed my cheek. "My queen, I will gladly give my life for yours, now and forever."

I smiled at his words. "Have you been rehearsing your wedding vows?"

Luca helped me up from the toilet seat. "We're getting married as soon as you feel better. No more waiting. I'm making you my wife."

My cheeks hurt from smiling so hard.

Marcello raised my shirt over my head while Bastian inched down my shorts. They made me change out of the wedding gown after I ate on the boat. I could tell just the sight of me wearing another man's dress made them want to kill someone.

Luca lifted me in his arms and carefully lowered me into the bathtub. Like I was as breakable as glass.

I leaned my head back on the tub and looked up at them. "Is this what to expect for our future? Never able to breathe, always having to watch our backs?"

Marcello sat on the tub's edge and tucked my curls behind my ear. "I won't lie to you, princess. Your life with us will never be easy. We have other battles to fight after we deal with Lorenzo and your mom."

Luca sank to his knees beside the tub. "Our business affairs attract the attention of dangerous men. But once you're my wife, they'll stop hunting you. Heirs and bastards are open season. But wives are off-limits. That's one rule no one in our world will break."

"They would have nothing to gain after you're married to us," Bastian added.

"No more lies," I said to them. "It took way too long for you to tell me about the auction and the Wellington dowry. There's so much I feel like I don't know."

"I thought I was protecting you." Luca raised my hand to his mouth and smacked another kiss on my skin. He hadn't stopped touching me since he'd gotten me back. "I'm sorry. I didn't want to upset you."

"Your mental health is our priority," Marcello interjected. "Blame me. It was my idea to keep the auction from you."

Luca reached across me to grab the body wash. "Sit back and relax. Let me take care of you."

I did as he asked, and Luca rubbed a soapy loofah down my arm. He was quiet the entire time he scrubbed my body. Luca wasn't a big talker, so I savored this moment with him.

Despite our differences, we were alike. I couldn't express myself as a child. But, my art and the stories I made up gave meaning to my life. Art helped me to understand how the world worked. It helped me cope with all the trauma.

All five of us had traumatic childhoods. I couldn't imagine losing one parent, let alone two. Yet, Bastian and Damian rarely spoke about their biological parents. It was as if they were always Salvatores. Like they hadn't had lives before moving from Bel Air to Devil's Creek.

Luca fisted my curls in his hand and kissed me, his lips soft against mine. He couldn't seem to keep his hands off me. Of all my men, he'd shocked me the most. Not that the others hadn't missed me and feared for my life.

But Luca was different.

Acting like a man in love.

I pulled him toward me, desperate for more, moaning into his mouth as I moved his hand between my thighs.

He kissed me harder.

When our lips separated, his breath fanned across my lips. "So impatient, my queen. You need to rest."

"Make me come." I shoved his fingers inside me. "I need to release this pent-up energy."

He sucked my bottom lip into his mouth, his fingers spreading me open. I rocked my hips, and Luca added another finger, kissing his way down my jaw and neck.

I spread my legs so my men could hover over the tub and get a better look. Damian pushed off the wall and licked his lips. His cock was already hard and poking through his pants.

Bastian moved to the ledge behind me and swiped my curls off my shoulder. "My sweet Cherry," he whispered.

Luca placed kisses on every inch of my body. "You make me lose my fucking mind. I will do anything to protect you. To keep you safe. To make you mine."

His fingers plunged deeper inside me, in and out, until I was screaming his name. My body trembled, my orgasm working its way through my body. As I chased my high, I'd never felt more alive.

"I'm yours," I moaned.

A ghost of a smile stretched across his beautiful lips. "Damn right, you're mine."

"All of yours," I clarified as I looked at his brothers.

Luca quickened his pace and bit my lip. And with that, I

came so hard on his fingers that my legs shook for a solid minute.

"I need all of you." I held out my hand and wiggled my fingers, aiming my gaze at Luca. "Take me to bed."

"To sleep," he countered.

Luca grabbed a towel from the rack and helped me out of the tub, cradling me against his chest. He kissed the top of my head and wrapped his arms around me. "Tonight, you're sleeping with me."

He was finally coming around. It only took a kidnapping for Luca to change his behavior.

Chapter Fourteen

ALEX

L uca wasn't thrilled about all five of us sleeping in his bed. He was a light sleeper and didn't want to share with his brothers. But he caved because he couldn't say no to me with all his guilt.

He felt like he failed me.

They all did.

I didn't blame any of my men for my kidnapping. None of them could have seen my mother coming. Her sudden reappearance was so unexpected. Even though thoughts of her still plagued me, I had tried to put her in the past. I tried to forget about all the horrible shit she had done to me.

It was time to move on and start a new life with my men.

Luca curled his arm around me, his blue eyes filled with desire. I loved when he studied my face like he was extracting all my secrets—peeling back each layer to see what made me tick.

He wasn't easy to read. Not when he guarded his heart and secrets, keeping them under lock and key. But he seemed to be coming around, more in tune with my needs and feelings. Especially after he found out about the baby. That seemed to mellow him out, provide him with some form of peace and security.

All five of us got into Luca's bed, stripped down to our underwear. Marcello rested my head on his chest, stroking his fingers through my curls. Luca was on my right, unable to take his eyes off me. Bastian and Damian sat at the end of the bed and watched us.

"We're going to need a bigger bed," I told them. "A California king isn't large enough for the five of us to sleep together."

Luca groaned. "Must we all sleep in the same bed? I prefer my privacy." His eyes drifted to each of his brothers. "And space."

"Me, too," Damian muttered. "You know how I feel about sleeping with people."

"You know I don't give a damn, one way or the other," Bastian chimed.

"Same," Marcello grunted. "Doesn't matter to me. I can sleep anywhere, as long as you're happy."

I smiled at him. "You're so sweet, Marcello."

"You don't like sweet." Luca stole me from his brother, so he could smother me in his warm embrace. "Our queen likes when we're savages." He nuzzled my neck with his nose. "Isn't that right, Drea?"

Leaning back on my elbows, I looked at each of them. "I love my savage Knights."

I grabbed Marcello's hand and moved it to my thigh. Then I took Luca's hand and placed it higher up my leg.

"What are you doing, Drea?" Luca sucked on my earlobe. "You need to sleep."

"I'm happy to be home with my guys." I looked at Damian and Bastian. "I need to feel all of you, so I know you're real. Because there was a time on the boat and the island when I wasn't so sure I would ever see any of you again."

Luca kissed my lips. "We would have burned down the world for you."

A smile pulled at my mouth. "I was counting on it." As I looked into his eyes, I wet my lips with my tongue. "Make me forget about the last twenty-four hours."

"You must be tired," Luca commented.

I stripped off my pajama top, throwing it across the room. "I know what I want, Luca. We can worry about everything tomorrow."

"Dr. Ferguson will be here in the morning to check on you and the baby."

I pressed my lips together and nodded. "Until then, let's forget about the island and the drama of our lives." I shoved his hand between my legs over the wetness seeping through my panties. "Touch me."

Marcello didn't waste a second. He grabbed his grandfather's knife from the nightstand and cut off my panties like a barbarian. He dropped the blade on the bed beside him and then sucked my nipple into his mouth. His fingers moved inside me, soft and gentle, until Luca shoved one of his fingers into me, working in unison with his brother.

They didn't usually touch me at the same time. It was one of Luca's rules. He wanted me all to himself and didn't want to share. But we were long past that stage. He knew it was all or none of us and had accepted his fate.

With his free hand, Luca cupped the side of my face and kissed me. I moaned into his mouth and yanked on the waistband of his boxers. Impatient and greedy, I was ravenous and desperate for more, unable to wait another second.

"Get naked."

"Not yet, baby." He pushed on my shoulder, pinning my back to the soft mattress. "Let us take care of you."

I fisted a chunk of Marcello's hair between my fingers, tugging at the ends. He stuck out his tongue and licked my nipple, his fingers moving alongside Luca inside me. Marcello teased me again, and I whimpered with each flick of his tongue.

"Marcello," I whispered. "Bite me." He did as I commanded, pulling on my nipple with his teeth, and my entire body felt like it was on fire. "Harder."

A rush of heat coursed through my veins and spread down my arms. Luca kissed my lips as Marcello made me scream.

"Luca," I moaned as he peppered my jaw with kisses.

I felt Damian and Bastian crawl toward us on the bed, the mattress shifting beneath their weight. My eyes immediately found theirs. They kneeled on the bed, their hard cocks in their hands, focused on me as they jerked their shafts.

I wanted all of them.

But I couldn't give each of them the proper amount of time with Luca and Marcello monopolizing so much of mine. I also didn't think I could handle all of them inside me tonight. Not after the beating my body had taken.

They took turns licking and sucking every inch of my skin until my body trembled. Damian leaned forward and kissed his way up my thigh. Bastian joined him, the two of them spreading my legs farther apart.

Luca pinched my nipple, and I cried out for more.

"Feel good, baby girl?"

I closed her eyes and lost myself with them. "Yes. Don't stop."

Pressing his palm to the mattress, Luca hovered over me, his breath ghosting my skin. I arched my back, lifting my hips off the bed, moaning into his mouth as his brothers devoured me.

My eyes snapped shut when Damian sucked my clit into his mouth. Then Bastian dragged his tongue over the tiny nub, fighting Damian for possession of me.

So they devised a system.

While Damian sucked my clit into his mouth, Bastian tasted every inch of me. I tugged on both of their short, dark hair, screaming their names and rocking my hips until I smothered them with my pussy.

As whimpers poured out of my mouth, my legs trembled, and one after another, I rode out my orgasms, coming hard and fast on Bastian's tongue. My men stared at me from between my thighs and licked their lips.

Still trying to catch my breath, I leaned back on the stack of pillows behind me, nestled between Marcello and Luca. With my men surrounding me, I'd never felt so loved and admired. Like a true queen claiming her Knights.

Luca cleared his throat, drawing my attention back to him. "You must be tired, baby."

I nodded.

He snaked his strong arm around me, rolling me onto my side. His hand moved from my breast to my stomach. "You're safe," he whispered into my ear. "You're loved." Luca brushed the tangled curls off my cheek. "Sweet dreams, *mi amore*."

Chapter Fifteen

ALEX

I awoke the following day to sunlight on my face. Blinking the sleep from my eyes, I sat up, my chest ready to cave from the wave of anxiety rocking through me. I thought I was still on the boat with Lorenzo for a second until I turned to the side, where Luca slept soundly.

I blew out a breath of relief.

This was my first time sleeping in Luca's bedroom. He'd never shared more than his body with me, and after all these years, his walls were crumbling down. My kidnapping made him realize what he could have lost.

Bastian, Marcello, and Damian were gone. Knowing Luca, he kicked them when I fell asleep.

Luca laid on top of the silky black sheets. I stared down at my sleeping devil, dressed in his usual black Dolce & Gabbana boxer briefs, shirtless and as handsome as ever.

I brushed his cheek with my fingers, kissed his forehead, and whispered, "I love you, Luca."

I'd never said the words aloud.

A moment of silence passed before he scared me half to death. He looked dead to the world a moment before. Then, his eyes popped open, the same pretty blue ones I had stared at hundreds of times. This wasn't how I planned to confess my love for him.

"You better love me," he said. "How did you sleep?" Luca looked at me with one eye open and curled his arm around me. "Are you feeling okay?"

"I'm fine," I assured him. "The medicine helped me sleep through the night."

I laid my head on his muscular chest, soaking up his warmth. Sucking his lip into my mouth, I placed my hand over his heart, feeling the steady beat.

He was real.

And all mine.

A smirk tugged at his mouth. "You said you loved me when you thought I was sleeping."

"It's true." My lips touched his. "I love you, Luca."

He slipped his fingers through my curls as his eyes met mine. "I loved my mom more than anything. And when I lost her, I never thought I would feel that way again. I thought I would spend the rest of my miserable life without caring about anything until I met you." His tongue slipped past my lips and tangled with mine. "I love you, Drea. I was so afraid of losing you that I pushed you away. I hated my feelings for you. I thought they made me weak and reckless."

"Love is unpredictable. You can't control it or contain it."

"Show me how much you love me." Luca moved me on top of him. "Ride my cock, baby."

Straddling his thighs, I fisted his cock through the slit in his briefs and shoved my panties to the side. I gave him a few strokes, and Luca groaned, his eyes meeting mine as I lifted my hips. His hand fell to my waist, fingers digging into my skin. I took all of him in one swift thrust, and my eyes shut from how quickly he filled me.

I leaned forward and pressed my palm to his chest, rocking my hips to meet his. Because I was in control, I wanted to make love to him. I took advantage of this moment and lost myself in him.

"Damn, baby," he grunted. "You feel so fucking good."

I gave him a cheeky grin. "You saying you missed me?"

He tugged on my hair in response.

As I kissed him, my body felt like it was on fire. I was so close, chills rolling down my arms as a wave of heat swept over me. Luca pumped his cock into me, taking control of our orgasms as they spilled out of us.

I came hard and fast, Luca right after me. We kissed long after our bodies stopped trembling. Luca threaded his fingers through my curls, crushing my mouth with a passionate kiss. Our tongues fought for power over the other as we deepened the kiss.

Everything was a game with us.

Neither of us would ever relinquish complete control, forcing the other to assert their dominance.

His hands slid down my back and over my ass, claiming me with the same hunger I craved. "I can't wait to marry you."

I smiled.

And then he was hard and inside me again, taking me to new heights, showing me exactly how much he missed me.

Chapter Sixteen

DAMIAN

L uca surprised Alex with a birthing room inside the mansion. We couldn't risk letting her off the property, so we'd decided she would deliver the baby at the house.

She covered her mouth with her hand as she walked into the room. "You guys, this is so thoughtful."

Alex rested her hand on the crib, and tears leaked from her eyes. Of course, Marcello was at her side, with his hand on her shoulder. My brother was always the first to comfort her. He knew what to do and say.

I couldn't even console myself, let alone another person.

How am I going to help a child?

On one side of the room was a king bed, a gynecological table on the other with a bunch of monitors. Luca ordered a ton of shit with the help of Alex's OBGYN. I didn't know a damn thing about babies and had never been around one.

From the moment Alex announced she was pregnant, I couldn't breathe. Just the thought of possibly being a father scared me to death. I'd feared nothing in my life, not until that day. We were terrified of raising a child, especially given the circumstances.

Marcello hugged Alex from behind as she stared out the

open patio doors that overlooked the bay. Bastian stood on her right, his fingers laced between hers. I wanted so badly to be there for her. But I didn't know how to be like my brothers. That part of my brain was missing.

"Dr. Ferguson will be here in five minutes." Luca shoved his cell phone into his jacket pocket. When Alex turned around, he added, "She's the best OBGYN on the East Coast. You're in good hands, Drea."

She slipped from Marcello's grasp and rushed to Luca, throwing her arms around his neck. "Thank you."

He kissed her pretty pink lips. "Only the best for our queen."

"We should talk about the paternity test." Alex angled her body to look at each of us. "Are you sure you want to do this?"

"Regardless of paternity," Luca said, "we won't treat them any differently. But we need to know for The Founders Society."

She dragged her teeth across her bottom lip and nodded. "To be completely honest, I'm kinda scared. I haven't felt like myself since my mother kidnapped me. I have these moments..." She released a deep breath, wrapping her arms around her middle. "I don't feel right. It could be the changes to my body from the baby. Or what happened on the island."

Luca pulled her into his arms. "It's okay, baby. Give it time. That was a traumatic situation."

She leaned back against his chest, her gaze on us. "I'm going to be a mother." Her eyes watered, and a single tear slid down her cheek. "It's freaking me out. I had a horrible mother. An even worse childhood."

Luca swiped at her tears and hugged her tighter. "You'll be a good mom, Drea."

"You will," Marcello interjected. "Because you learned what not to do."

Bastian took her from Luca and kissed her forehead. "You

have nothing to worry about, Cherry. This baby will love you as much as we do."

Dr. Ferguson cleared her throat as she entered the room. "Gentleman." She lowered her head and then smiled at Alex. "Hello, Alexandrea. I'm Dr. Ferguson."

She was tall, probably close to six feet, and had long auburn hair. A dusting of freckles dotted her pale skin. Somewhere in her late forties, she was one of the best in her field and specialized in different birthing techniques. Luca chose her in case something went wrong with the birth. My brother had accounted for every variable. He'd researched babies and birthing and everything you didn't even want to know about childbirth and parenting.

He tried to convince me to read a few books. I wasn't ready. It still didn't feel real that one of us was the father of her child.

As expected, Marcello and Bastian dived right into the material. Bastian had cared for me for most of my life, so I already knew he would be a good father. He could put his own needs aside to help others, as he had done for me more times than I could count.

Both of them would be excellent fathers. Even Luca would be better at it than me. We were the most alike, both of us unable to process emotions, especially those of others. But he was getting better with Alex. Slowly, my brother was becoming a different man.

Alex hopped up on the table. With the doctor on her left side, there was only room for one of my brothers on her right. Marcello nudged Bastian out of the way and held her hand. Bastian stood beside him with his hand on Alex's knee.

Luca moved next to me and lowered his voice. "Is this too much for you?"

I shook my head. "No, I'm okay."

"Alex needs all four of us," he said in a hushed tone. "We need you, too. So you better fucking snap out of it." His deep voice became more menacing. "Read the fucking books I gave you. Try fucking harder." His teeth clenched as he spoke. "Because if you do anything to upset or push her away, I won't let you near her or the baby."

I turned to look at him, my body trembling from the anger shaking through me. "You can't keep me away from her."

"I don't want to hurt you, Damian." His jaw ticked as he looked at me. "But if you don't get your shit together, I won't have a choice. I've spoken with Bash and Marcello about this. They agree."

"Bash would never agree to that," I snapped, accidentally raising my voice, drawing everyone's attention to me.

Alex glanced at each of us. "Is everything okay?"

Luca held out his palm and forced a smile. "It's okay, Drea. We're just talking." Then he tipped his head to the doctor. "Proceed with the ultrasound."

The doctor nodded and went back to work.

Our girl stretched out her hand and wiggled her fingers. "Damian, come here. I want you to see the baby."

The baby.

A new life.

I had only ever taken lives. Creating one still felt like such a foreign concept to me.

Because I was obsessed with her, even possessed by her, I closed the distance between us.

She took my hand and laid it on her stomach, a big smile on her face. "It's okay to be scared, Damian. I am, too."

Luca moved to the end of the table, his unwavering gaze aimed at Alex. We waited as Dr. Ferguson lifted Alex's shirt and rubbed a clear gel onto her stomach. I heard the heartbeat before I saw the image on the screen.

That was a sound I knew well.

When you take a life, it's the last thing you remember. The sound of their heart thumping in their chest when they realized it was almost over. I felt my heart racing a mile a minute, my entire body shaking. Alex noticed and looked up at me. Thankfully, she said nothing.

Our baby moved on the screen. It was so tiny—a little Salvatore boy or girl.

"You're eleven weeks," Dr. Ferguson confirmed. "The baby looks healthy. But we'll run some tests since you were concerned about the drugs you've taken."

"I didn't take them," Alex corrected. "Someone injected me with them."

Dr. Ferguson nodded. "I'll run a few tests, but I think they will come out just fine. The heartbeat sounds good. I don't see any signs of concern."

"Can you tell the sex?" Luca asked.

"Not yet." She gave a slight shake of her head. "Between fourteen to eighteen weeks."

"How soon can you determine the paternity of the baby?" Luca said in a firm tone.

"Right away," the doctor lilted. "I will draw blood from each of you and conduct a fetal cell analysis. It's non-invasive and won't hurt the baby."

The Founders Society needed to confirm the baby was a Salvatore by blood.

Dr. Ferguson printed out copies of the ultrasound for each of us. I held the image of the baby in my shaky hand, unable to control my racing heart.

Bastian must have sensed my distress because he moved to my side and clutched my shoulder. "You can do this, D."

Luca didn't have faith in me and brought my worst qualities to the surface. While he fed my demons, Bastian tried to keep them at bay.

After the doctor took blood samples from us, she left the room, promising to send the results.

Alex sat on the bed between Marcello and Bastian. Luca was on his knees in front of her, touching her stomach. I couldn't stop looking at the picture in my hand.

The baby was real.

"No peeking at the paternity results ahead of time," Alex said to Luca. "I want to open them together."

Luca raised her hand to his mouth and kissed her skin. "I promise, my queen."

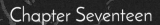

Chapter Seventeen

LUCA

I stalked Alex on the security feeds and watched Marcello exit our mother's studio. He was outside of the room, talking to the guard. After a few minutes alone, Alex dropped her paintbrush on the tarp and rose from the floor. I thought she would go after Marcello since they were so fucking co-dependent.

Instead of following my brother, she walked over to the wall with all of my mother's paintings. She pressed her palm to the wall and stood there in complete silence, taking in each detail of the piece.

Her lips moved as she leaned closer to the painting that made my mother a star. The Truth About Liars. Alex loved the painting and often quoted my mother.

Her fingers glided across the wall as she strolled down the row of paintings. She stopped in front of my mother's self-portrait and started speaking. I hit a button on the screen to get the audio in the room and turned up the volume.

"You would be so proud of them," Alex said in a hushed tone. "They've come a long way." She smiled so widely it reached her pale blue eyes. "Luca is so strong and smart, a natural leader. He's always in control, and that makes me feel safe. I like that about him, even though it used to scare me. And Marcello…" A dreamy look washed over her face. "He's such a good man. The way he takes care of me."

Alex leaned against the wall, turning her head to the side as if my mother were beside her. "The way he loves me… The way both of them love me." She hugged her middle and smiled again. "I love them. And I will take care of them for you."

My lips parted in shock.

Alex spoke to my mother as if she were inside the painting. Was she fucking losing her mind? Had the kidnapping fucked her up more than she was telling us?

I hadn't expected her to snap back right away. Not after all the trauma she'd endured in her life. But speaking to a painting of a dead woman was not sane.

She pushed off the wall and returned to the tarp, gripping the paintbrush between her fingers. I raced downstairs to the second floor and told Marcello to take a lap before entering my mother's studio.

Alex was on her stomach with her butt in the air, the paintbrush gliding across the canvas. I loved watching her work. She looked so free and in her element. My mother had the same look when she painted as if nothing mattered while creating another masterpiece.

I stopped in front of her, my hands stuffed into my pockets. She looked up at me with a sexy smile gracing her full lips.

"Stop staring at me." She pointed at the armchair beside her. "If you're going to linger, sit and stop hovering over me."

"Hovering is what I do best."

"Sit or leave." She waggled her eyebrows at me. "Make your choice."

I laughed at her feistiness. No one but Alex could tell me what to do and get away with it.

"We both know who is in charge in this relationship." I

dropped into the chair beside her. "But I hear marriages take compromise to work."

"They do." She sat up and put her palms on her thighs, those pretty blue eyes aimed at me. "So you better learn how to share the power in this relationship."

I smirked. "Whatever you want, my queen."

"You've been saying that a lot lately."

I reached out and touched her cheek. "I'm happy to have you back. But is there something you need to tell me?"

Her eyes narrowed. "No, I don't think so. But, unlike you, I don't keep secrets."

"No more secrets," I promised.

"Why do you think I'm lying to you?"

I dropped my hand from her face and leaned forward. "Because you said you were okay. But I watched you talk to my mother's painting on the security feed."

She tipped her head back and laughed. "You saw me?"

I nodded. "I heard what you said."

"I'm not losing it," she assured me. "I talk to your mom all the time. We're besties." She giggled, flicking her curls over her shoulder. "Marcello knows I talk to her. He caught me a few times. Sometimes, he talks to her, too."

I shook my head and laughed. "Crazy and beautiful. I guess I can't get one without the other."

"Don't tell me you haven't talked to her."

"It's different." I shrugged. "She was my mother. I knew her."

"Her art speaks to me the way a song would for others. I don't need to hear her words to understand her." She scooted closer to my chair and moved between my legs. "The first time I saw one of her paintings, I cried. It was so beautiful... It was like she understood my pain."

I dabbed at her tears. "She would have loved you."

Alex rubbed at her eyes and smiled. "When my grandfather adopted me, I was so excited to meet the sons of my favorite artist. But you were so… vile." She breathed through her nose and swatted at another fallen tear. "Well, we won't go into the past. But I was so upset, not just because you were mean to me. I thought you and Marcello would be more like your mom. I thought the sons of an artist would be less… What's the word?" She tapped her index finger on her lips. "Less uptight."

"I'm not uptight."

Her laughter filled the air. "Yes, you are, Luca. You're so serious all the time."

"I'm trying," I confessed.

"I know." She licked her lips as our eyes met. "I'm so proud of you and all the progress you've been making. That's what I was telling your mom."

I leaned forward and kissed her sexy lips.

Alex climbed onto my lap and hooked her arms around my neck. "I'm so horny," she said between kisses, grinding on my cock. She shoved her shorts and panties to the side. "My hormones are so out of whack."

"I'm good with that." I sucked her lip into my mouth. "You can ride my cock all day, baby."

She reached between us and unzipped my pants. Her hand trembled as she touched me, so I moved her hand away and took control.

I gripped her hip and fisted my shaft. "Sit up, baby."

Alex lifted her hips so I could fill her in one quick thrust. She fell forward and hooked her arms around my neck.

"Are you okay, Drea?" I slid my hand beneath her chin to look into her eyes. "You're not acting like yourself."

"I'm fine." Her hands moved to my shoulders, digging into my back. "Shut up and fuck me."

I grabbed her ass cheeks and rocked into her hard enough to leave an imprint of my cock. "Is this what you want, dirty girl?" I pulled on her curls, and she whimpered. "Huh? Use your words."

She licked her lips. "Yes, yes… Harder." Several moans slipped past her lips as her movements matched mine. "Oh, my God, Luca. I love your big cock."

I fucked her as hard as she liked it, pulling out and slamming back into her with force. "Yeah, baby? Tell me what else you love about me?"

Before she could answer, Marcello entered the studio. The door shut behind him, drawing Alex's attention to him. He groaned as he watched us and scrubbed a hand across the dark stubble on his jaw.

I turned her head to face me. "Look at me. Not my brother." I tugged on her bottom lip with my teeth, and she moaned. "Cum all over my cock, pretty girl."

"Marcello," she whimpered. "Touch me."

My brother moved behind Alex and massaged her big tits, licking her neck. We were too close for comfort. Threesomes were Damian and Bastian's thing. No fucking way in hell I was letting Marcello slide in the back while I fucked our girl.

Nope.

Never.

My brother tilted her head back and kissed her lips. "You look so fucking sexy right now." His teeth grazed her jaw. "I could devour you, princess."

I was so close, on the verge of losing it, as her pussy squeezed my cock. She came hard and fast, scratching at my back as my brother teased her. And it wasn't long before I was chasing my high, spilling my cum inside her.

Marcello stepped backward, and I pulled her closer, pecking at her lips. I sucked her lip into my mouth, and she tugged on mine.

My cell phone rang, cutting through the silence. She sat back with a groan as I reached into my pocket.

It was my dad.

I raised the phone to my ear. "Yes."

"Round up your brothers and come to my office."

He hung up without another word.

I shoved the phone into my pocket and looked up at Marcello. "Dad wants to see us in his office."

My brother lifted Alex off of me, so I could tuck my dick into my pants. Some of our cum dropped out of her pussy and onto my slacks. When I tried to wipe it away, it smeared on the fabric.

"Fuck."

"You don't have time to change," Marcello told me.

I shook my head and sighed. "Yeah, I know."

My dad hated tardiness.

I rose from the chair and smoothed a hand down the front of my pants. Alex stood beside me, biting her lip as she looked at me.

"Duty calls." I bent down to kiss her lips. "Paint something for me."

"Will you be gone long?"

"I don't know, baby."

"Benji will sit with you while you paint," Marcello said. "And you'll have two guards at each end of the hallway. I'll send Benji in after we leave." He lifted her feet off the floor and kissed her. "We'll be back soon, princess. Two floors above you."

I glanced down at Alex's canvas on the tarp and smiled. She drew a group of men wearing cloaks with hoods over their heads. The man at the center of the group had eyes that shone various shades of red and orange, while the others had X marks over their eyes.

"What gave you this idea?" I asked her.

"It's The Devil's Knights. After all of you saved me from the island, I realized how much this queen needed her Knights. You couldn't have rescued me without their help."

I pointed my finger at the canvas. "Why did you cross out their eyes?"

"For anonymity." Nonchalant, she rolled her shoulders. "Since it's a secret society."

I raised an eyebrow at her. "Why are my eyes different?"

She laughed. "Who says that's you?"

"Please, Drea. We both know the man at the center is me."

"I want to reveal the painting at my next showcase since the Russians ruined the last one."

"You sold out the Blackwell Gallery," I reminded her. "It was still a success."

"I sold out because the four of you bought the paintings."

I snickered at her comment. "Like we would let a stranger hang our faces in their homes."

Alex walked with us across the massive room. "I'm working on other pieces. One of them is a surprise. A wedding gift to the four of you. I painted it for our eyes only."

I waggled my eyebrows. "Sounds kinky."

She laughed. "It's more suggestive than my usual work. We can hang it in my bedroom."

"I want it now."

"Good things come to those who wait, Mr. Salvatore," she taunted.

Chapter Eighteen

MARCELLO

I sat in the chair across from my father with a glass of scotch. He puffed on a cigar, the smoke filling his office. Luca sat on his right while Bastian and Damian took their usual places beside him.

My dad flicked the ash onto the tray on the coffee table. "The auction ended last week. Lorenzo is still on the run with Savanna. Our intel confirmed he has the support of The Lucaya Group. They're hiding him in New York."

Damian's nostrils flared.

The Lucaya Group was a sore spot for my brothers, and rightfully so. They killed their parents.

Bastian shot up from the chair, enraged by the announcement. "I'm done waiting to take them down. You promised us revenge fifteen years ago." He balled his hands into fists at his sides, his top lip quivering. "We handed over twenty-five percent of Atlantic Airlines for The Founders Society's connections. Damian and I have waited too long to get close to The Lucaya Group."

"I have every intention of following through on our agreement," he assured Bastian. "We're not backing down from The Lucaya Group or Lorenzo Basile."

My brother hovered above my dad's chair, so angry he spit as he spoke. "You promised you would help us find these bastards. This is our chance. We finally have enough allies."

Dad clenched his hand on the arm of the chair, holding Bastian's fiery gaze. "They're the same people who have tried to steal Battle Industries' artificial intelligence software. Drake is in danger. This is a precarious time for all of us. You will get everything I promised you, Bastian." He pointed his finger across the room. "Now, take your seat and let me finish."

Bastian stepped back, his eyes wandering around the room as if it had just hit him that his outburst was unnecessary and aimed at the wrong person. My dad had adopted Bastian and Damian when they had nothing left. He gave them a home and a family and welcomed them into The Devil's Knights. We never treated them as if they weren't Salvatores by blood.

"Sorry." Bastian loosened his silk tie. "I'm just... frustrated."

"It's okay, son." He tipped his head at the couch. Bastian sat, and then my dad continued, "There's a lot at stake. First, we have to locate Lorenzo and Savanna and neutralize the threat. Once the new head of the Sicilian family is in place, we will work with our Mafia counterparts to bring down The Lucaya Group."

The Lucaya Group had disappeared from the map fifteen years ago, with only a few random appearances over the years. And once they vanished, they were untraceable. Considered the best in the business, they were a terrorist organization funded by the deepest pockets in the world. But we could draw them out of hiding using Bastian's cousin.

She went by the name Grace Hale, but she was born Katarina Adams Romanov. Grace was the only living granddaughter of Fitzgerald Archibald Adams IV, Bastian's grandfather and the leader of The Founders Society.

"Get Drake on the phone." Luca aimed his attention at me. "See if he can dig up intel on Lorenzo using his AI software. I'm sure someone on the Dark Web is talking about what went down on the island."

I removed the cell phone from my pocket. Drake was the same age as Luca, but we'd grown closer over the years. We were both into technology and liked poking our noses into places they weren't supposed to be. He'd taught me how to hack, though I wasn't near Drake's level.

My fingers glided across the keys as I looked at my father. "We need to move the wedding up."

"About that." His gaze moved between us. "Did Alexandrea choose yet?"

"Yes," Luca cut in. "She chose all of us. But she will marry me."

His left eyebrow rose a few inches. "Do you expect me to let my sons share the same woman?" He shook his head. "I'm not okay with this arrangement."

"You don't have to be," Luca shot back. "We didn't intend for this to happen. But Alex wouldn't agree to marry me if she had to choose between us."

His nose wrinkled in disgust. "I raised the four of you better. Your mother would roll over in her grave."

"I don't think Mom would have cared," I said in our defense. "As long as we are happy."

He knew I was right and ignored my statement. "Carl will not approve of the wedding if all of you declare your intention to marry her."

"She'll marry me," Luca confirmed. "That's all anyone outside of this family will ever know."

Dad looked at me and shook his head. "I expected more from you, Marcello." Then he moved to Damian. "I always knew you wouldn't live a normal life, not with your illness."

"I can't let her go," Damian told him, with a stern expression hardening his dark features. "She's the only woman who understands me."

He nodded his acceptance.

None of us had expected Damian to have a normal relationship. Not with all of his emotional and mental baggage.

Dad moved to Bastian. "You're an Adams. There are certain rules for men like you. Fitzgerald won't allow you to be with Alex while she's Luca's wife."

"I don't give a fuck what Fitzy wants," he fired back, irritation dripping from his tone. "The old man can go to hell. I'm sick of him trying to dictate my life."

"The carrier is on their way to the house with the paternity test results." Luca shoved his cell phone into his pocket. "We'll know soon which of us fathered the child."

Dad let out another disgusted groan and stiffened in his chair. "It better be yours, Luca. Or we're going to have a lot of explaining to do."

Chapter Nineteen

ALEX

It was the moment of truth. As Luca held the envelope in his hand, my entire body trembled with a strange mixture of fear and excitement. While everyone lounged on the couches in the sitting room, Damian looked like he was ready to jump out of his skin.

"Do you want to do the honors, my queen?" Luca handed me the envelope and made room for himself on the couch beside me.

Bastian placed his hand on my thigh. I could tell he wanted so badly to be the baby's father. Marcello, too. They both had this hopeful look in their eyes. Luca didn't seem like he cared one way or the other, but it wasn't easy to read him. He was a lot like his father in that regard.

Damian paced in front of me, biting the inside of his cheek as he wore down the floorboards. He was tense all afternoon and even worse at dinner. Because he knew the carrier was on their way with the results.

I slid my trembling finger beneath the fold of the envelope. It felt like the longest second of my life as I removed the paper and unfolded it.

My heart leaped out of my chest when I found his name. I

clutched it against my chest and looked at each of them. Then my eyes fell on Damian until he stopped moving and glanced down at me.

Reading the truth from my face, he shook his head. "No." He kept shaking his head. "No, I can't be…"

"You're the father, Damian."

Luca took the paper from my hand and read it thoroughly, inspecting the DNA analysis.

I stretched out my hand. "Damian, come here."

He stared at my fingers as if they were diseased. My heart broke for him as I watched the wheels turning in his head. He thought the darkness inside him meant he wouldn't be a good dad.

"Please, Damian." I wiggled my fingers. "I need to know you're okay."

He tugged at the ends of his black hair and sighed, turning away from me. "No, I'm not fucking okay!"

His sudden outburst caused Bastian to stiffen beside me. I could feel them going into battle mode as they read Damian's body language. It looked like he had gone to another place, deep inside his mind. His green eyes looked even darker than usual and narrowed into slits.

Bastian shot up from the couch and inched toward him. "D, we talked about this." He held out his hand. "Alex is carrying your baby. It's okay to be scared. None of us know how to do this. But we'll do it together."

As Bastian advanced on him, Damian turned away from us. Bastian tried to grab hold of him, but before he could latch onto his arm, Damian stormed out of the room.

"I'm going to snap his fucking neck," Luca growled through clenched teeth. He hopped up from the couch with Marcello. "I warned him not to fuck this up."

Bastian and Luca attempted to go after him, but I yelled, "No, leave him alone!" I got up from the couch and moved in front of them. "It has to be me." I pushed out my palm.

"Let me talk to him before you do something you will regret."

"I won't regret smashing his head into the fucking wall." Luca bared his teeth. "He's not ruining this for you, Drea. I won't let him."

I hooked my arms around Luca's neck, pressing a kiss to his lips. "I got this, Luca. I can get through to Damian."

"You don't have to baby him," Luca challenged. "He doesn't deserve your attention for running out on you."

"Luca, I don't expect you to understand."

"No, I don't. You should be mad at him. "

"Just let her go," Bastian cut in. "They have their way of sorting things out."

"That's not how we handle shit in this family," Luca said. "Damian needs to get on fucking board."

"I will handle him," I assured him. "Pour yourself a glass of scotch and calm down."

Bastian laughed at my suggestion.

Breathing through his nose, Luca dropped into the armchair and waved his hand. "Go after Damian. But if he hurts you, I'm going to kill him."

"He won't," I said with absolute certainty.

Marcello tipped his head, telling me to go. He understood I needed to do this alone. I couldn't reach Damian with Luca yelling at him.

And here, I thought Luca was making progress. Maybe he was just angry he wasn't the father and resented Damian.

I took one last look at them and headed down the hallway. My search of the first floor was uneventful. So I headed upstairs to the second floor and went straight to his bedroom.

I found Damian flat on his back, staring at the ceiling with his dress shoes dangling off the bed. If the others had acted this way, I probably would have beaten the shit out of them. But because it was Damian, and I knew he was different, I wasn't as mad as I should have been.

I strolled into his bedroom and sat on the mattress beside him. "I'm not mad at you for running away, Damian. I understand this will take some time for you to adjust." I slid my hand across the duvet and placed it on his thigh. "But I need you to be here for the baby and me."

When he sat up, I noticed he had a picture in his hand. It was the ultrasound image Dr. Ferguson had printed for each of them.

His eyes flicked between the image and me. "I'm not capable of love," he whispered. "I don't know how to do this." He shook his head, unsure of himself. "I won't be a good father."

I climbed onto his lap and straddled his thighs. "The fact you're worried about being a dad tells me you're going to be good at it."

Damian gave me a weary look. "How do you know that?"

"A shitty father wouldn't care if he was bad at it." I laced my arms around his neck and brushed my lips against his. "Damian, I love you. And if I can fall in love with you after all the horrible shit you've done to me, then this baby will love you even more than I ever could."

His hand cupped the back of my head, and he pulled my lips closer to his. "Do you think so?"

I nodded. "I know so."

"What about when I lose control?" He sighed. "A child can't be around me... Not when I'm like that."

"I think this child will change you in ways you never expected." I sucked his bottom lip into my mouth. "I think your heart will be less black the moment you see your child. And I think one day, you will realize you love us." I rubbed my hand over my growing stomach. "Because I know you are capable of love. I see it every day with Bash. You love him. You love all of us, even if you can't process the words."

His hand covered mine. "I can't feel the baby."

"It's too soon." I moved our hands in a circular motion

over my stomach. "But you'll be the first person I tell when I feel the baby kick."

In one swift motion, Damian had me on my back, his muscular body pinning me to the mattress. His lips hovered over mine. "I feel very possessive of you," he confessed. "Obsessed with you. Those two emotions I understand well."

"I love both things about you." I shoved my hand through his dark hair and pushed it off his forehead so I could look into his pretty green eyes. "I love how you watch me and can't seem to get enough of me. Growing up, I never felt wanted. You make me feel more desired than anyone I have ever met."

He lifted an eyebrow. "Even my brothers?"

I bobbed my head. "It's different with you. I can't quite explain it." I hooked my legs around his back, and his hard cock poked my inner thigh. "You used to scare me when you looked directly at me. Your expression was so intense, like a hunter. But I no longer feel like your prey, Damian."

A sadistic smile tugged at the corners of his mouth as he stroked my cheek with his fingers. "I enjoy having you at my mercy."

"I'm here willingly," I pointed out. "When I hop into bed with you, I know what I'm getting myself into and no longer fear you."

He inched my shirt up my stomach and bent down to kiss my skin. I couldn't help but notice he spent more time on my belly, which made my heart swell with love for him. Of course, no one expected him to get used to being a father overnight. We all knew he would have the most challenging time with it, so I mentally prepared myself.

Damian's lips moved lower, stopping at the waistband of my shorts. His tongue darted beneath my panties, teasing me with each flick of his tongue. I slipped my fingers through his hair and encouraged him to keep going.

He ripped off my shorts and panties and licked me straight down the center. I loved when he tasted me. It was like he was making love to my pussy, taking his time to savor every second.

After I came on his tongue, he glanced up at me, his lips glistening from my cum. He kissed my inner thigh and winked. "Good girl, Pet."

Chest heaving, I reached between us and yanked his tie. "Get undressed, Damian."

He didn't waste a second, flipping open each of the buttons on his oxford and removing his pants and boxer briefs. I took in the sight of him naked and licked my lips.

His tattoos started at his collarbone and stopped below his belly button. Both arms were thick with muscles and had sleeves of ink, leaving very little of his pale skin untouched.

He ripped off my shirt and flung it across the room. I placed my hand over his heart, right over the black script that said Alexandrea with a crown beneath it. Even if he didn't see it, he loved me. Why else would he have gotten my name on his chest?

Damian leaned forward and pushed inside me. I thought he would be rough, like usual, but he surprised me by making love to me. It was nice. So different from other sexual experiences with Damian.

He stopped moving and looked into my eyes. "Can I hurt the baby?"

"Is that why you're taking it slow?"

He nodded.

"You're not hurting me." I touched the side of his face and smiled. "And, no. I don't think you can hurt the baby."

Damian took that as a green light and pumped into me harder.

"But I liked what you were doing before." I ran my hand down his back and felt a few of his scars. "Can you do that for me?"

"I would do anything for you, Pet." He bent down and

parted my lips with his tongue, kissing me softly. "You're mine." His hand brushed my stomach. "Mine."

I enjoyed seeing this side of Damian. It was still carnal and raw but so fucking sweet. Rocking my hips to meet his, I kissed him back, craving every second of our lovemaking. I came again, my orgasm shaking through him, each of my moans turning into screams of pure pleasure.

His right hand crept up to my throat, and his pace quickened before he spilled his cum inside me. He released his grip, still on top of me. "Tell me you're mine."

I put my palm over his heart, feeling the strong but rapid beat beneath my fingers. "I'm yours, Damian."

Chapter Twenty

ALEX

I stood on the front steps of the Salvatore Estate, waiting for my brother to arrive. We hadn't seen each other since we left the island.

Sandwiched between Marcello and Bastian, I realized this was now my home. Only a few months ago, this place felt like a prison. But with the wedding day approaching and a baby on the way, it was time to settle into my new life.

Aiden parked his cherry red late sixties Mustang in front of the garage. He was well over six feet tall and clean-shaven, though his wild curls flopped all over the place. Wearing a pair of khaki shorts and a black button-down shirt, he strolled toward me with a smile.

"Did you join a boy band?" I joked, surprised by his unusual attire. "You look like you've just fallen out of an Abercrombie & Fitch ad."

He tipped his head back and laughed. "Pops made me wear this for a meeting."

"That explains a lot."

I met him halfway and launched myself into his arms. A mixture of mint and laundry detergent lifted off his skin, and I drank in his scent.

Tears welled in my bottom lids as I looked up at him. "How are you healing?"

He held me at arm's length and stared into my eyes, a warm smile stretching across his face. "It was just a flesh wound. A few stitches. I'm good as new."

"That's good." I touched him to make sure he was real. "I'm so happy to see you."

I glanced over at my men, who kept their distance. Marcello gave me a genuine smile that touched his eyes. Even Luca had a slight grin tugging at his mouth. Since we got home, he smiled more, which he rarely did before my kidnapping.

Bastian held my gaze, arms folded over his chest, while Damian stood beside him with his hand shoved into his pockets. He liked to watch me. Observe me in the strangest ways. But I liked that about him. With Damian, I felt seen.

"How have you been?" Aiden tucked my curls behind my ear. "Mom and Lorenzo put you through hell. Are you sleeping okay?"

I rolled my shoulders. "Some nights are better than others. When I have nightmares, Bash or Marcello can usually get me back to sleep. I'm taking it one day at a time. That's all I can do."

"Anytime you need me, I will be there."

I touched his face, needing to feel his warmth on my fingertips. "What about your initiation?"

"I'm staying with Pops until your wedding. Then I go back to the safe house for three more months." Aiden clutched my wrist and studied the diamond ring gleaming on my finger. "I'll be home before you have the baby."

"How about a drink?" Luca asked my brother. "We have a few things to discuss before the seamstress arrives."

I slipped out of Aiden's arms and into Luca's, walking into the house with my men. The six of us sat on the back veranda, which overlooked the bay. Luca was on my right, my brother on my left. I squeezed both of their hands and held them on top of my knees.

My stomach growled loudly.

Luca glanced down and spoke as if he were talking to the baby. "Are you hungry?"

I rubbed my hand over my belly. "I think she's hungry."

♛♛♛

After eating lunch, a beautiful woman with an Italian accent brought my wedding gown to the house. I couldn't let the guys see my dress, so I'd asked Aiden to stay and hang out with me.

He was going to be my man-of-honor.

I had no friends. My parents didn't allow us to interact with kids at school. And no one wanted to talk to us, anyway. So even in Devil's Creek, we were still outcasts, despite our family's status. It was always the two of us until my men entered the equation.

I changed out of my clothes behind a dressing screen. Domenica walked out of the room, promising to come back in a few minutes to give us some privacy. I slipped into the gown and stepped out from behind the screen for Aiden to zip me.

Luca told me I could have any dress I wanted. So I sketched something no one would ever wear, something so unique it would look stunning in wedding pictures. Like something straight off the runway.

He hired one of the top designers in the world to work around the clock to bring my vision to life. The dress had black feathers with a long train and a low-cut corset.

It was as I had envisioned.

"Wow," my brother muttered as he appraised my dress. "You look like…"

"A black swan," I finished for him.

His mouth widened as he ran his hand over the feathers in awe. "You sketched this? It's brilliant."

I tugged at the dress and smiled, still in awe of my vision coming to life. "I can't take all the credit. The designer did an incredible job."

Domenica entered the room a minute later, her mouth wide with surprise. "Stunning." Her eyes roamed over each of my curves. "You don't need any alterations. It fits perfectly."

After I changed, Domenica took the dress. "I'll bring it back the night before the wedding," she said before leaving the house.

Aiden walked with me onto the veranda, where all four of my men smoked cigars and drank from highball glasses. They looked happy, at peace, as if the world's weight had lifted off their shoulders.

My mother and Lorenzo were still on the loose. So were the Russians and the men who helped my mother kidnap me.

But for today, they could relax.

We had a lot to celebrate.

Chapter Twenty-One

BASTIAN

Alex woke up screaming from a nightmare. Our girl tried to put on a solid front, but she still wasn't herself. There were brief moments where she panicked or forgot where she was, only to snap out of it a few minutes later.

"Damian," she whimpered with her eyes closed. "Damian, come back. Don't leave me."

She often called out for each of my brothers between fever dreams. Last night, it was Marcello. The night before was Luca. Both nights, they got into my bed with her, but she was so out of her fucking mind she didn't even know they were in the room with us.

I lifted my cell phone from the nightstand and texted Damian. It was three o'clock in the morning. Like me, he was a light sleeper and never slept more than a few hours a night.

A minute later, my bedroom door creaked open. He stood in the entryway shirtless and wearing a pair of black boxer briefs. My brother rarely wore anything with color, not unless you counted gray.

He scratched the dark stubble on his jaw. "Is she awake?"

"No." I set the phone on the table. "She's calling out for you, D."

He shut the door and closed the distance between us.

"She needs you." I patted the mattress. "Get in."

Damian climbed into the bed, and she stirred when he shoved the curls off her cheek to get a better look at her face. "I don't want to wake her. She looks so peaceful."

I tipped my head. "Say something to her. Hearing your voice may help."

Damian lifted her in his arms and rested her head on his chest. His fingers wove through her curls in a loving, soothing gesture that was so foreign to him. But, lately, it seemed like Damian was changing.

When I'd first suggested he see a therapist, I prayed it would work. I hoped for his sake that something would click in his brain. But that never happened.

Then Alex came along.

Because of her, I got to witness these moments of intimacy. Damian didn't know how to console himself, let alone someone else who was hurting. Our father had taught us that weakness would get us killed. He showed us how to endure the pain but also taught Damian how to embrace it for his deviant purposes.

He cradled her face with his hand and dipped his head to whisper in her ear. "Wake up, Pet."

"Louder," I urged.

"Pet," he boomed, going from one extreme to another.

"No!" She swatted her hand at his chest. "No! I don't want to leave."

"Maybe speak in a normal voice." I shook my head. "Yelling upsets her."

Damian dragged the pad of his thumb across her bottom lip. "Can you hear me, Pet?"

She whimpered again and rocked back and forth. Damian grabbed her hands and held them to his chest so she couldn't hit him again. My brother glanced over at me with sadness in his green eyes.

"This isn't working," he groaned. "She's more like Eva than we thought." He slumped back on the pillows and held her. "Do you remember the manic episode she had the month before she died?"

I nodded. "It took Dad two weeks to get her out of bed."

"Carl gave her something. We need to find out what it was, so we can give it to Alex."

"She's pregnant, D. Eva took some hardcore meds when she was on a bender. I doubt they would be safe for Alex."

He shrugged. "It's worth a try."

"Like you, Alex has a mental illness," I reminded him. "None of us have ever forced you to be someone else. So we won't do that to her."

Damian narrowed his eyes at me. "Fuck, I didn't mean it like that, Bash. I don't want her to change… I wish I didn't feel so fucking useless."

"She will struggle with this for the rest of her life," I pointed out. "Carl thinks she's going to have issues throughout her pregnancy because of her high cortisol levels."

"How do you do this?" His eyebrows lifted as he looked at me. "With me, I mean. You've been going through this shit with me since we were kids. What's the secret?"

I considered his question for a second. "Patience. I realized a long time ago I couldn't fix you. Most of the time, you can control yourself. Alex can do the same as long as she's not pushed too far. We need to be here for her and let her figure this out on her own. She's a prisoner in her mind right now."

Damian moved his hand to her stomach. Alex let out a soft purr like she knew he was here, even in sleep.

"Keep going," I insisted.

His hand dipped beneath the waistband of her silky pajama shorts. "Time to wake up, Pet. Your Master commands it."

Alex wrapped her fingers around his wrist and pushed his

hand lower. "Damian." Eyes closed, she licked her lips. "Damian, please."

He sucked her earlobe into his mouth, and she rolled her head to the side, giving him better access. "Do you need to come, Pet?"

Her eyes snapped open. Alex stared up at him and then glanced over at me. She grabbed my hand and rested it on her thigh.

"How are you feeling, Cherry?" I shoved the sweaty hair off her forehead and kissed her skin. "Are you in there, baby?"

"Yes," she whispered, her gaze shifting between Damian and me.

She gripped both of our hands. "I want to feel both of you."

I kissed her lips. "Tell me what's going on in your head."

"Help me forget."

She pulled the pajama top over her head and threw it across the room. Alex moved our hands to her big tits, helping us massage her nipples.

I twisted her nipple, ripping a moan from her mouth. "Are you sure this is what you want, Cherry? You've been asleep for a long time. You need to eat."

Her gaze shifted between us, and then she shook her head. "I'm not hungry for food."

Damian rolled onto his side, so he could suck Alex's nipple into his mouth. I kissed her as my brother made her squirm with each flick of his tongue.

She moaned into my mouth and yanked on the waistband of my boxers. Impatient and greedy, she was ravenous, like she couldn't wait another second. I clutched her shoulder and pushed her back to the mattress.

Alex licked her lips, tugging on Damian's hair as he stuck out his tongue, peeking up at her as he licked her nipple. She whimpered when he did it again to tease her.

We were trying to go easy on her. After everything she'd

been through, she needed to rest. She also needed to eat and take her vitamins. I could already see myself being possessive of her the entire pregnancy. Marcello was usually the one who babied her, but I was slowly falling into that role.

I crushed her lips with a kiss as Damian dragged his teeth across her neck. We took turns kissing, licking, and sucking on her skin. Our pretty girl trembled with need, desperate for a release.

I inched down her body and sucked her nipple into my mouth. Damian covered the right side of her body in kisses, working in unison with me. He wasn't usually so careful. But she was changing each of us in different ways.

Impatient, Alex took my hand and pushed it down her panties. "Bash, please stop torturing me. I won't break if you touch me."

"We are touching you, Cherry."

She groaned. "You know what I mean."

I pulled her panties down a few inches. Damian licked his lips, his nose tipping up at the scent of her desire.

Working in unison with Damian, we tore off her panties. She wanted both of us, so we thrust our fingers inside her. Our sexy girl loved it when we tag-teamed her. She was so tight and wet, so ready for us.

I was dying to be inside her.

As we fucked her with our fingers, moans slipped past her pretty pink lips. I stuck out my tongue and rolled it over her clit. Alex arched her back, lifting her ass off the mattress.

"I want both of you," she whimpered.

I glanced at Damian, and then his tongue brushed mine as we licked her pussy. We'd never kissed before. This was the closest we'd ever come.

With Damian, I didn't have many boundaries. I let him push all of mine. It was the same with Alex. Whatever she wanted, I would give her without a second thought.

She moaned as we devoured her. Her eyes slammed shut

when we took turns sucking her clit into our mouths. Damian licked between her slick folds, desperate to taste every inch of her. So I focused on her clit, nibbling and licking until my sweet cherry tugged on the ends of my hair, screaming our names.

Whimpers of ecstasy poured out of her mouth. Her legs trembled, forcing us to hold her down. Then, one after another, she rode out her orgasms and came on our tongues.

I stared at her from between her spread thighs and kissed her soft skin. Damian clutched the back of her thigh, licking his lips as he committed her naked body to memory.

Leaning on her elbows, she looked at us with her chest rising and falling with each breath. "I want more."

I pressed a few kisses on her inner thigh. "Tell us what you want, Cherry."

We were hers to command.

A glimmer of excitement illuminated her pale blue eyes. "I want you two to kiss."

Chapter Twenty-Two

ALEX

B astian stared at me, unblinking for a moment, and then his eyes shifted to Damian. From the moment I saw them together in the shower, I wanted them.

I got on my knees between them, tugged on the waist-bands of their boxer briefs, and licked my lips. I turned my head to look at Bastian. "Kiss me."

His lips crashed into mine, his tongue sweeping into my mouth. He stole the air from my lungs, each kiss more passionate than the last, consuming every inch of me. When our lips finally separated, I struggled to catch my breath. Bastian tucked a curl behind my ear, a smile in place as his gray eyes met mine.

I hooked my arm around Damian's neck and pulled him closer. He bit my bottom lip, sucking it into his mouth before kissing me like he wanted to eat me alive. I was hoping my sexy prince would do just that.

Panting, I peeled my lips from his and then pushed my guys closer to each other. Bastian assumed I would think differently about him for having feelings for Damian. But it only turned me on and made me crave them even more.

Damian didn't bother to hide how he felt about Bastian. I

once thought it was just a brotherly bond until that night in the shower.

I kissed Damian again, then Bastian, before moving back just enough to allow their lips to brush. They breathed hard, most of the hesitation on Bastian's part. My heart raced with each second I watched, waiting for them to give in to their desires.

I knew Damian wanted this.

The two of them had gone much farther than a kiss, so it surprised me Bastian was the holdout. His fingers curled around Damian's throat as he looked into his eyes, still breathing hard and fast.

Damian stuck out the tip of his tongue and licked Bastian's lips. The sudden connection was enough for Bastian to lower his guard, his resolve fading. And then he kissed Damian without an ounce of hesitation on his part.

Their kiss was angry and hot, the two growling like feral animals as they squeezed their hands around each other's throats. Damian reached between them. He yanked down Bastian's boxer briefs, jerking his cock in long strokes that drove him wild. A little pre-cum wet Damian's hand. His movements were quick and precise, as if he'd done this to Bastian hundreds of times.

They had a perfect rhythm.

Like they knew each other's bodies as well as their own. But, unlike last time, Damian was the aggressor. He shoved Bastian onto the mattress, climbed on top of him, and ripped off his boxers.

My heart pounded like a drum, ready to punch its way out of my chest. I slipped my hand between my thighs and rubbed my clit. Bastian looked over at me as Damian sucked the tip of his cock into his mouth. His eyes closed for a split second, and he let out a hiss.

He raised his hand and beckoned me with his finger. "Come here, Cherry." Bastian patted the space on the bed beside him. "Sit on my face." His hand moved to the back of Damian's head as he took him into his mouth. "Let me taste your pussy, baby."

I didn't waste a second and straddled his head with my thighs, facing Damian, so I could watch. He jerked Bastian's shaft while he sucked his enormous cock.

Placing my hands on Bastian's chest, I leaned forward and kissed the skin below his belly button. I inched my way lower, sticking out my tongue to get a taste. My tongue touched Damian's as I repeated this motion.

"Fuck," Bastian groaned and drove his tongue inside me, eating my cum like he was starving.

He gripped my ass cheeks and licked me from front to back, leaving no part of me untouched.

My skin pebbled with tiny bumps, the chills spreading down my legs. I put my hand over the top of Damian's, and his eyes met mine. Bastian's cock popped out of his mouth, and then we both went to town, taking turns licking and sucking.

Teasing and tasting him.

I fisted Damian's black hair in my hand, our tongues tangling as we fought for possession. Bastian smacked my ass while he licked me. Making me come so hard and fast that I thought I saw stars.

He ran his hand over my right cheek, spanking me repeatedly, easing the pain until every sensation turned to pure pleasure. I moaned his name when he shoved his fingers inside me and sucked my clit into his mouth. Then he inched a finger into my ass, spreading me open.

My orgasm slowly built until it reached its crescendo. And as I sang his praise, Bastian's legs trembled. Damian jerked his shaft as we both leaned forward, our mouths open. His intense green eyes met mine as cum coated our lips and tongues.

Groans of ecstasy escaped from Bastian. We swallowed his

cum, and then licked his skin, kissing each other in the process.

My dark prince swiped his thumb across my lips, a crazed look dancing across his face. I could tell he was going to tear me apart. And I wanted whatever sick and dirty punishment he had in mind.

Damian snaked his arm around me and, in one quick movement, flipped onto his back so he could pull me on top of him. His cock was inside me within seconds, filling me to the hilt. I glanced over at Bastian. He was semi-hard and could probably go another round.

I raised my index finger and beckoned him. "Fuck my ass, Bash." I licked my lips and moaned as Damian ripped through my inner walls, taking me with force. "I want to feel both of you inside me."

Bastian rolled onto his side and grabbed a bottle of lube from the drawer beside his bed. He moved behind me, straddling Damian's thighs, and smacked my ass. "Ride my brother's cock, dirty girl." Then his hand whacked my skin again. "Mmm… Look at you, Cherry. You're so wet your thighs are slick with your cum." Another smack. "Does seeing us together turn you on?"

"Uh-huh," I moaned. "More than anything."

"Squeeze my cock, Pet." Damian dug his long fingers into my hips and fucked me like a savage. I followed his command, tightening my muscles around him. "That's it. Harder." I listened to his order, and he praised me as if under his spell. "Good girl."

Bastian rubbed his hand over my ass and eased the ache as he helped me fuck his brother.

I felt his breath on my neck, and a rush of heat shot down my arms. Then, with his finger slick with gel, he plunged it inside me, sliding it in and out until my body adjusted. A wave of heat and then cold rushed over me.

After Damian made me come, Bastian removed his

finger and replaced it with his cock. I gasped as he moved inside me, taking his time. He always let Damian fuck me from behind. But he felt so damn good. My head spun, drunk with pleasure and the intoxicating smell of sex in the room.

"Bash," I bit out. "Oh, my God."

Then my eyes dropped to Damian, who looked up at me with his lips parted, his chest rising and falling with each deep breath. Bastian grabbed my breast, massaging my nipple with the rough pad of his thumb. A moan slipped past my lips, on the verge of another orgasm.

"My sweet Cherry," Bastian whispered into the crook of my neck. "Fuck, baby, you feel so good."

"Damian," I screamed, pressing my palms to his chest as I moved my body in unison with them. "Bash. I'm so close… Oh, God. Yes, yes, yes!"

Bastian fisted my curls in his hand and tilted my head back to kiss my lips. "Cum for us, Cherry."

An earth-shattering orgasm swirled inside me, ripping through my body like a hurricane. I held onto Damian while Bastian hooked his arm around me, claiming my ass as he pinned me to his brother's chest. Damian's cock jerked inside me, and then he was filling me up, making me feel so damn full.

After we both stopped shaking, Bash pulled out, and his warm cum splashed across my ass cheeks. He hopped off the bed and grabbed a wet towel from the bathroom to clean me up.

Exhausted, he dropped onto the bed beside Damian. Looking up at the ceiling, he covered his heart with his hand.

Damian moved me to the mattress between them. Naked and dripping in sweat, the three of us breathed in unison, still high from that delicious encounter.

"I think the two of you will be my death. I've never come that many times in a row."

Bastian turned onto his side and bit my bottom lip. "You're such a good girl."

Damian grunted his agreement and patted the top of my head. "Good Pet."

Bastian's fingers wove through my messy curls that were all over the place. "You have to eat and take your vitamins. It's not healthy for the baby for you to be sleeping all day and night."

I felt like shit when he put it that way. Since I got back from the island, I had moments where I was not okay. They gave me pills prescribed by my grandfather, which helped during my episodes. But I needed to snap out of this funk.

"I want soup, nothing too heavy."

Bastian lifted his phone from the nightstand and texted the kitchen. No matter the day, someone was always around to attend to their needs. I didn't think I would ever get used to staff waiting on us.

I looked over at Damian. "Will you stay the night with us?"

He nodded. "If you call out my name again in your dream, I'll be right here."

I smiled. "I dream about you all the time, Damian."

"Oh, yeah?" He smirked. "Dirty dreams, I hope."

I waggled my eyebrows, giving him a playful smile. "Stick around and find out."

I put my hand on their chests and brushed my fingers over the scars that marked each of them. Then, with my head turned to the side, I looked at Bash. "You said you would tell me how you got the scar over your heart."

"I told you. Damian gave it to me."

"There's no point in hiding from me," I shot back. "Not after what we just did together."

"I guess you could say I was one of Damian's first victims," Bash confessed.

"What?" I stared at him, eyes wide. "You mean the X over your heart... So he tried to kill you?"

"Not exactly." Damian turned me onto my side and hugged me from behind. "I wanted to practice my skills." His breath fanned across my neck. "Bash volunteered as tribute."

Laughter shook through me. "Are you kidding?"

His big hand brushed my stomach in slow, circular motions. Since he'd gotten used to being a father, he often touched my belly. He asked every day if I could feel them kick, even though it was too early.

"Half the scars on Bash's back and chest are from me."

"I assumed they were from your dad."

"Some of them," Bastian confirmed.

"So why an X?" I asked Damian. "You could have chosen anything."

"Because I wanted Bash to remember our past." He kissed my neck, causing my skin to pebble with goosebumps. "It's a reminder never to feel how we did back then."

"But meeting you changed everything for us." Bastian brushed his fingers down my arm and smiled. "We love you. And we want to feel everything with you."

Chapter Twenty-Three

ALEX

L uca knocked on the door before popping his head into the bathroom. As he approached me, I stood in front of the mirror, fixing a loose curl into a diamond pin. Licking his lips, he stopped a few inches behind me, dressed in his usual armor—a black suit that fit his muscular body like a glove. I wore a white Roman-style dress that swept over one shoulder with golden accents and a long slit down my right thigh.

"Your family is arriving soon." He cupped my shoulders, staring at me in the mirror with a seductive look in his eyes. "You look divine. Like a goddess." His fingers trailed down the length of my arm, leaving fire in his wake. "If we had more time…" He kissed my shoulder. "The things I would do to you, my queen."

I chuckled. "We don't have time."

He kissed my neck, then my jaw. I leaned back against his chest, drinking in his delicious scent.

"I'm a patient man, but the wait is killing me." Luca buried his face in my neck, peppering my skin with kisses. "I don't want to wait for another second to make you my wife."

He pressed his lips together, and a worried expression darkened his handsome features.

"What are you not telling me, Luca?"

"Lorenzo is on the move." Luca rubbed my shoulder as he stared at me in the mirror. "He was last spotted in New York. Drake's been monitoring him."

"Why are the Luciano brothers helping you? Aren't they Lorenzo's nephews?"

He nodded. "But they don't answer to the Sicilians. Dante and his brothers run Atlantic City. Most of their profits come from gambling. They're not into guns and drugs."

"Lorenzo sells drugs?"

"He strong-armed the Knights into transporting guns and drugs for him using Mac Corp containers. But we refused to help him traffic women."

"Your dad turned Salvatore Global into a multi-billion dollar empire. So why do you keep working with the Mafia and drug cartels?"

"It's not that easy to walk away. We have a long-standing relationship with our clients and know too much about their illegal operations."

"Which makes you a liability if you walk away."

"Exactly." He spun me around and backed me onto the counter. "We don't have a choice, baby. If I could get out of these deals, I would." He tucked a curl behind my ear. "Having powerful friends is useful to us."

"What do you mean?"

"Lorenzo is ruthless," he said in a stern tone. "And not well-liked in Italy, not even among his men."

"Are they planning a coup?"

He bobbed his head to confirm. "Dante has been in contact with Lorenzo's second-in-command, Giovanni Angeli. They're working together to move against Lorenzo. That's why he left Italy. He suspected his men were plotting against him."

I expelled a deep breath, relieved by the news. "When is this going to be over?"

"Soon, baby. I promise." He stroked my cheek with the rough pad of his thumb. "Once we're married, he won't have any reason to take you from us."

"Luca, what's going to happen to me?"

"Nothing, baby." He bent down and kissed my forehead. "I will gladly give my life for yours."

"No, you can't. I won't allow it."

He grabbed my hand and covered his heart with my palm. "Do you feel this? My heart only beats this way for you. You are a part of me, Drea. Without you, none of this shit matters. My life doesn't matter."

"Luca, don't say that."

"You revived me." He shoved his hand through my hair and kissed my lips. "I was drowning in a sea of darkness, and then you saw me. The real me. You accepted my scars and pain, and I knew you understood. You saved me, baby girl. I'm not a good man, and I never will be. But the part of you that lives inside me is good. And I save those parts of myself for you and only you."

A knock on the door caused me to jump. Sudden sounds sent my heart racing into overdrive.

Marcello poked his head into my room, dressed in a black suit with a gold tie. "Dad wants you downstairs before the Wellingtons arrive."

"We'll be down in a minute," Luca told him.

After Marcello left, I stared at Luca, memorizing every detail of his gorgeous face. His moments of vulnerability were so rare I wanted to soak them up.

"One of us will always be with you, no matter what," he said to assure me. "We won't let you out of our sights."

"I wish we got to spend more time alone." I inched my hands up his muscular chest and wrapped my arms around his neck. "You're always so busy."

His fingers wove through my curls as our eyes met. "I can't be with you every second of the day. I'm running a global company. My family relies too much on my expertise."

"I still don't understand what you do for Salvatore Global."

"I'm the Chief Operating Officer."

"I get that. But what exactly do you do?"

He rolled his shoulders. "On the books, I'm in charge of the company's daily operations. I handle interactions with VIP clients and coordinate business dealings with American and foreign governments. I'm also in charge when my father is unavailable."

I cocked an eyebrow at him. "And off the books?"

"I map trade routes throughout the world to move illegal products."

"So that's what you do all day and night in your office? Map trade routes."

He shook his head. "It's complicated. I have to jump through legal loopholes to get around certain issues. It's not black and white. I operate more in the gray area."

"Thank you for being honest with me." I reached up to press a kiss on his lips. "I always ran from you because you never opened up to me. I never felt like I had a place in your heart."

"You do." He kissed me again. "Always."

We entered the formal dining room. The Salvatore men sat behind a long table with Arlo at the head. He reminded me of a king overlooking his courtiers. Damian and Bastian sat on their father's right side, with Marcello on his left. They were engaged in what sounded like a heated discussion before they heard my heels click on the tiled floor.

Luca flung out his hand. Then, without a word, his brothers moved down two chairs to their right to make room for us. After Luca pushed my chair into the table, he took his place at his father's side.

A server poured wine into his glass. Luca raised it in front of his nose, swirling the liquid as he took a whiff of the grapes. His family owned vineyards across the United States and Italy. One of their many legitimate businesses served as a funnel for illegal activities. I drank ginger ale, which helped with the random bouts of sickness.

Five minutes later, the butler announced my family. My grandfather entered the room in a bespoke black suit with a crisp white oxford and a black tie. Blair was at his side, dressed to the nines in a black designer gown fit for a runway.

I smiled as my eyes locked with Aiden's blue ones. He wore a black suit and tie, his curly blond hair cut shorter than the last time I saw him. His face brightened from the smile that stretched the corners of his mouth.

I rushed over to Aiden and flung myself into his arms. "You look so handsome." I touched his cheek. "No more peach fuzz."

Next, I hugged my grandfather. "Hey, Pops."

He kissed my cheek and hugged me back. "Hello, princess. It's good to see you back to health."

We still weren't on the best of terms after he revealed the truth about our families. But he was the only parent I'd ever had. He took care of Aiden and me and gave us opportunities we wouldn't have had without him. Despite our differences, I loved him. He was still my grandfather.

"Our children are getting married," Arlo said to my family as he stood at the table's head. "We have a lot to discuss." Arlo cleared his throat, his gaze on my grandfather. "After the past month's events, we must take certain precautions."

My grandfather and Arlo dealt with the wedding. They

had every aspect figured out. I didn't care about the semantics. I just wanted to marry my guys and become Mrs. Salvatore.

"As for Alexandrea's shares in Wellington Pharmaceuticals," Arlo said in a deep tone, drawing my attention back to him. "They will transfer to Luca after the wedding."

What shares?

He made it sound like our wedding was purely transactional. Like I was nothing more than a pawn to move around a chessboard. Maybe at first, it was a business deal between our families. But over the past few months, I'd fallen in love with each of them. So this wedding was real in every sense.

I glanced at my grandfather. "How many shares do I own?"

Pops set his snifter down on the table and turned his gaze to me. "You and Aiden each own twenty-four and a half percent of the company. I own fifty-one percent. When I die, you and Aiden will inherit everything."

My lips parted in surprise. "And Luca will get all of my shares?"

"Yes, but he's not allowed to sell them. It's part of the deal I struck with Arlo. The shares will pass to your children."

I left the topic alone and assumed my grandfather had my best interest at heart. It didn't matter if Luca owned a portion of my family's company. He would be my husband soon. All four of them would officially be mine.

"To the start of a brilliant partnership between the founding families." Arlo raised a glass, stealing everyone's attention back to the head of the table. "To Luca and Alexandrea."

Chapter Twenty-Four

DAMIAN

Midway through dinner, all of our cell phones dinged with a new message. It was the group chat with Drake Battle and the local Knights.

Drake Battle: We got Savanna and one of Lorenzo's men. Meet us at the safe house on 5th.

I glanced over at Bastian and Luca. They pushed out their chairs from the table. Marcello was next to rise to his feet. With a nod in my father's direction, I followed my brothers and excused myself from the table. All four of us left the ballroom without a word.

Alex's heels clicked on the marble floor behind me. She tugged on my suit jacket sleeve. "What's going on?"

I turned to face her. "Drake found your mother and her boyfriend."

Her eyes widened. "I'm going with you."

"Stay here," Luca shot back. "Let us handle this, baby. You're safer at home."

"No." Alex gritted her teeth. "She kidnapped me and sold me to a Mafia boss. That bitch tortured me and starved me for most of my childhood. I want revenge, too. You can't take this from me."

She was right.

I called out Aiden's name. He rushed into the hallway with a doe-eyed look. The Wellington heir wasn't Knights material, despite his legacy as a Founder, but he'd proved himself useful. After the wedding, he would return to his post to finish his initiation into The Devil's Knights.

"Fine," Luca groaned. "You can come, but you need to change out of your dress." He tapped her on the back. "Take Aiden with you."

Without a word, Alex turned on her heels, holding Aiden's hand as they walked down the hallway.

"What are we going to do with Savanna?" I asked Luca, who had been planning to kill her for years.

At one time, he wanted to kill Alex. He took out his anger over his mother's death on our girl. But all three of us fought him. Even I didn't want to see any harm come to her. Not after I touched her, tasted her. I would have slit my brother's throat if he had put his hands on her.

"We need to find out who hired her," he said. "Then we can get rid of the bitch."

"Witnessing this could trigger another episode from Alex," Marcello cut in. "I don't think she should see us torturing her mom."

"It will be therapeutic." Luca grinned like a maniac. "Maybe it will give her some closure."

After Alex changed into black yoga pants and a red tank top, she met us at the entryway, still holding Aiden's hand. I'd never spent much time around her twin. He seemed okay, a little too soft for my liking, but he was protective of our girl.

So he was okay in my book.

We piled into the Escalade, and Marcello drove us to the safe house in Beacon Bay. No one spoke the entire ride. I stared out the window, watching the dark sky pass us by as I thought of all the ways I wanted to torture the people who kidnapped our girl.

Marcello parked in front of the apartment building in Beacon Bay. This place was like a second home to me. Over the years, I slept on the floor in the apartment beside a body. Still covered in blood, my heart racing, my cock as hard as steel.

Sometimes, Bastian couldn't reach me. I was too far gone, consumed by the bloodlust. Like the night I choked Alex and almost killed her. I still hated myself for hurting her, for making her fear me. But she no longer trembled when she saw the darkness inside me.

Alex climbed out of the car and turned her head to look at me. "Does anyone live here?"

"No." I gripped her elbow and steered her toward the front door. "We use it as a safe house."

She flicked her blond curls over her shoulder. "How many of those do you have?"

I rolled my shoulders. "A lot."

She narrowed her eyes at me.

"I've lost track," I admitted. "We have safe houses across the United States and in every country we do business."

Her right eyebrow rose an inch. "To kill people?"

"Depends on the situation."

"While you were in art school," Luca cut in, "There were a few months when we had to move between safe houses to keep the drama from our illegal businesses out of Devil's Creek."

Drake emerged from the lobby, dressed in dark jeans and a black fitted tee. The Knights had been running on fumes for the past week. None of us could sleep until we handled the threats against my family.

"I prepared the room for you." Drake looked at me. "How do you want to handle them?"

"Wait!" Alex's hand shot into the air. "Are you going to kill my mother?"

"We need to get information out of her first," Luca said. "Then you can do whatever you want with her."

Her mouth widened as her gaze flicked between us. "I don't know what I want."

Aiden clutched her shoulder. "If you can't do it, I will."

"Not if I beat you to it," Luca challenged.

Alex waved her hands between them. "Okay, can we not talk about killing people like it's normal?"

"This is business." Luca crossed his arms over his suit-clad chest. "We will eliminate anyone who poses a threat to our family."

"But…" Alex bit her lip, thinking over her response before Luca cut her off.

"Your mother handed you to Lorenzo for money." He uncrossed his arms and invaded her space, towering over her. "She didn't care about you when you were born, and she doesn't care about you now. She's hurt all of us. And if we let her live, she will continue to pose a threat." His palm moved to her stomach. "You have a baby to think about, Drea. I wouldn't put it past your mother to hurt our child."

"The baby is yours?" Aiden asked.

Alex looked at me. "No, it's Damian's."

For a split second, Aiden looked disgusted. But when he saw the murderous expression on Luca's face and mine, he forced a smile.

Drake turned his back to us. "Follow me."

We walked down a dimly lit hallway and upstairs to the apartment. Drake pushed open the door to reveal Savanna and her accomplice tied to chairs at the center of the living room. He'd even spread out an array of torture devices for me on the kitchen island.

Alex froze when she saw her mother, who had aged little over the years. They could have passed as sisters, with their long blonde curls, pale blue eyes, high cheekbones, and full lips. Savanna was thinner than Alex, with bony arms and legs and zero definition in her body.

When Alex moved to Devil's Creek, she mirrored Savanna's lithe frame. You could tell her mother had starved and abused her.

I tapped Alex on the back, forcing her to move into the room. I wasn't sure if she could even do this, but I wanted to give her the chance to get her revenge. There was nothing I wanted more than to cut her mother into tiny pieces for permanently scarring our girl.

Savanna tried to yell, but the bandana covering her mouth muffled her screams. Her companion knew better than to fight us. He slumped to the side, his face bruised and dripping blood.

Alex's eyes swept over to the weapons on the kitchen island. Drake had gathered a collection of guns, knives, ropes, chains, and surgical tools. She gripped the edge of the counter, studying each weapon carefully.

I moved behind Alex and slid my hands to her hips. "Choose one."

She bit her lip. "I hate her, but I don't think I can hurt anyone."

I swiped her curls off her shoulder and kissed her neck. "In this room, you're the judge and jury. We'll be the executioners."

Alex lifted a scalpel from the table. "How would you use this?"

Eyes wide, Savanna struggled against the restraints binding her to the chair. Even if Alex didn't want to kill this bitch, I would gladly help her mother leave this world.

I took the scalpel from Alex's hand. "This could take all night, a slow and painful death."

"Get what you need from her," Alex said in a hushed tone. "I don't care what happens next."

A sick grin tugged at my mouth.

Chapter Twenty-Five

ALEX

I couldn't move from the kitchen island, frozen in place at the sight of my mother. Even after years apart, she instilled the same fear inside me. My head pounded, and my vision slightly blurred as I attempted to focus.

She didn't deserve a reaction from me. But I couldn't control the emotions sweeping through my body. Lately, I felt everything, not just the sensitivity in my nipples and the rest of my body.

Emotions poured out of me. Some days, I felt like I was losing control. The trauma of the kidnapping and the island stuck with me. And despite my guys and their best efforts, I still wasn't myself.

I kept taking the pills Pops had given to Luca. Most nights, I needed them, or I couldn't sleep. Bastian and Marcello were the best at comforting me. I could usually fall asleep if I were in one of their beds.

Bastian clutched my shoulder. "Are you okay, Cherry?" When I didn't respond, he waved his hand in front of my face.

The sight of my mother sent a shiver down my arms, bringing back all the painful childhood memories.

The locked closets.

Pounding on doors.

Aiden yelling.

My screams.

Her laughter.

Marcello wrapped his arms around me from behind and kissed my neck. "We can go home if this is too much for you."

Home.

That sounded good. But I couldn't run away and let my men handle everything. They wanted a queen, so it was time for me to get my shit together.

Why was it so hard?

I could feel reality slipping out from under me. It took little to push me over the edge.

"Do what you have to do," I whispered. "I'm fine."

Luca rushed over to my mother and the dark-haired man tied to the chair beside her. One of Lorenzo Basile's men. He was still on the run with the help of The Lucaya Group.

Damian held a scalpel and stood beside Luca, staring down at my mother. His eyes flicked between each of his victims. I didn't have it in me to take a life. And since he enjoyed it so much, I wanted Damian to be the one to do it.

But they both needed this, especially Luca, who had planned his revenge for the past fifteen years. She had killed his mother for no reason other than jealousy.

A life for a life.

She owed him.

Luca bent down, ripped off the gag, and squeezed my mother's throat. "Who hired you to kidnap Alex?"

She gasped for air, her eyes wide as she looked up at him. When she didn't answer him, he tightened his grip. Swatting at his hand, she begged him to let her go.

Not so tough now, Mother.

For the first eighteen years of my life, she bullied me. Treated me as disposable. We looked so much alike that, at one point, I couldn't even look in the mirror. It was another reminder of her. My mother was beautiful and flawless, and she had given me most of her best features. I'd always wondered if that was why she hated me so much.

Did she see me as a better version of herself?

Luca lifted her off the chair, squeezing her throat. "Answer me, bitch. Or I will make this a slow, painful death. We'll drag it out for weeks. Make you wish you'd chosen the easy way."

As his one hand dropped from her throat, she coughed, struggling to catch her breath. "No, please." She gasped, her chest rising and falling with each breath. "Don't. Kill. Me."

"Then answer my fucking question," Luca shot back.

"A man approached me," she choked out. "He said he would give me five million dollars if I kidnapped Alex from your estate."

"What's his name?"

She shrugged. "He used a nickname. Mr. Fitz."

He folded his arms over his chest, glaring at her. "What did he look like?"

"Older but not quite his age," she muttered. "Wealthy. He dressed like my father. Even wore the same brand of aftershave."

Luca turned to look over his shoulder at Bastian. "Pull up a picture of your grandfather on your phone."

Bastian removed the phone from his pocket, shaking his head. He couldn't believe his grandfather had anything to do with my kidnapping. But when he showed my mother the image, she nodded.

"That's him," she confirmed.

"Fucking Fitzy." Bastian crushed the phone in his palm. "That motherfucker."

"I told you not to trust him," Damian added with a sneer. "He's a fucking snake."

Luca pushed out his palm between them. "We'll deal with him later." Then he turned back to my mother, his face as expressionless as marble. "If Fitzy paid you to take Alex, how did you end up on Lorenzo Basile's boat?"

"Because that old bastard double-crossed me. He only used me to get into the catacombs. He had no intention of paying me."

Luca smirked at her response. "Do you know why he wanted to trade Alex?"

She bobbed her head. "For the Wellington black book. My father has something on him. And he wanted to burn the book."

Rich people.

My life was worth more than a stupid book.

Luca hovered over her with a frightening expression on his face. "Let me get this straight. Lorenzo was going to marry Alex to get the black book and hand it over to Fitzy?"

"Yes." She rubbed her lips together. "That would be my guess. He didn't exactly share his plan with me. But he was desperate to get the book. So he tracked me down, thinking I could get it from Wellington Manor."

"You could have done that instead of kidnapping Alex," Luca fired back, his anger radiating off him in waves.

"No." She shook her head. "The black book isn't at Wellington Manor. And it's not a book. It's a data storage drive."

His eyebrows rose. "Where is it?"

"In a vault in Switzerland," she confessed. "I don't know which bank."

Luca walked away from my mother and stopped in front of me. Teeth clenched, he looked at me, then to Bastian and Marcello. Damian moved to his side, waiting for him to speak.

Lowering his voice, Luca said, "If the drive is really in Switzerland, Fitzy will wait for Carl to retrieve it."

"I doubt my grandfather would travel to Switzerland for it," I pointed out. "He has people who do that for him."

Luca shook his head. "It's too valuable. He'll go himself."

"Which means your grandfather is also in danger," Marcello said. "Fitzy probably already has teams following him, waiting for him to make a move."

"This makes sense why we could never get ahead of the situation with Russians," Bastian said with anger in his tone. "My grandfather has been working against us."

"I told you something was off with The Founders Society," Luca countered. "With their help, we could have captured the Russians. We could've had Alex removed from the Il Circo website."

Bastian scratched at the corner of his jaw and sighed. "I can't believe he did this."

"I can," Damian grunted. "I've been telling you for years. There's something not right about him. And that's saying a lot coming from me."

Marcello snickered. "We need to talk to Dad. Taking on Fitzy before the Founders admit us into the society will fuck up our plans."

Luca nodded in agreement.

Damian pointed his finger at my mother and her accomplice. "What do you want to do with them?"

"Keep them alive until we talk to Dad," Luca confirmed. "Carl may want to speak with Savanna before starting a war."

"Carl has everything to gain with Fitzy out of the way," Marcello said. "He could have been involved with the kidnapping."

"My grandfather is a lot of things," I said in his defense. "But he would never sell me to a Mafia boss."

"He sold you to us," Luca said in a flippant tone that made me want to smack him across the face.

"Don't talk to me like that, Luca! I'm not a stock or a piece of art. I am not and never have been for fucking sale."

He held out his hand, and I stepped back from him.

"You know I didn't mean it like that, Drea."

Bastian curled his thick arm around me and kissed the top

of my head. "We didn't buy you, Cherry. A woman as special as you is invaluable."

I smiled. "Even if I were for sale, you couldn't afford me."

He laughed. "That's what makes you so special."

Luca pulled me out of Bastian's arms, sliding his fingers down my arms in a soft, soothing motion. "You're irreplaceable. One of a kind. Like the Mona Lisa."

I smiled at his sweet comparison. "Nice save. But talk about me like our relationship was a transaction again, and you'll see just how cold this ice queen can be."

"So vicious." He kissed my lips. "One of the many reasons I love you." Then he pointed at my mother and her accomplice. "I'll deal with those two." His gaze turned to Marcello and Bastian. "Go back to the house and talk to Dad. See what he wants us to do about the Founders."

"I'll stay with you," Damian offered.

"Me, too," Aiden chimed.

"C'mon." Marcello clutched my hip and guided me toward the door. "You and the baby need to rest."

Before we left the room, I knew I would never see my mother again. I stopped to look at the woman who had haunted my nightmares for years. A pleading look spread across her face like she thought I would help her.

Not a chance.

I squeezed Marcello's hand, my eyes on her. "Goodbye, mother. May you rot in fucking hell, where you belong."

Chapter Twenty-Six

BASTIAN

After we spoke with Carl, he confirmed he had to increase his security detail because of his issues with my grandfather. We had the upper hand for now.

Fitzy didn't know we captured, tortured, and killed Savanna and her boyfriend. That she told us all of his dirty secrets. With that bitch out of the way, we had to dispose of another unnecessary family member.

Damian sat in the passenger seat beside me and clenched his fist. He hadn't spoken a word since we got into my Porsche. Visiting the last place we wanted to go had us on edge.

"D," I said when we were down the street from the house. He turned to look at me, and I continued, "It's going to be okay. You hear me?"

He nodded.

"We'll get in and out. Marcello will disable the security system. No one will even know we were here."

Another nod.

"Don't let him fuck with your head," I fired back. "He's not allowed to win. Do you hear me?"

Damian had gone full-blown mute on me. Not the fucking

time for him to get lost in his head. I needed my brother to be on his A-game with my grandfather. You could never lower your guard around Fitzgerald Archibald Adams IV. He would sniff out the weakness and use it against him.

The vein in my neck throbbed as we approached my grandfather's mansion in Sagaponack. I wanted to kill him. Wring his fucking neck for conspiring with Savanna to kidnap Alex. That old bastard was ruthless and only cared about one thing—money.

For a brief period after our parents' deaths, Damian and I came to live with him. But, unfortunately, it was the worse month of our lives. We went from living in Bel Air with our parents, doing whatever the fuck we wanted, whenever we wanted, to being treated worse than rats.

That month with Fitzy changed Damian.

Something inside him snapped when we went to live with the Salvatores. I blamed my grandfather for turning Damian into a monster. He beat us, tortured us, and locked us in the dark basement without food for days. He refused to send us to school or even let us shower.

Alex didn't know how well we understood her pain, how much we could relate to her panic attacks. We'd lived in the dark for so long we might as well have been born in it. That was the sad part. After that, we got used to it being the two of us, only needing each other.

It was one month.

But enough to change us.

I couldn't even imagine years of what Alex had endured at the hands of her mother.

After the month, Fitzy made a deal with Arlo Salvatore, and we started our new lives. The first six months with Eva were pure fucking torture. She didn't physically hurt us, but the daily threats to call child services had us living in fear constantly.

When Luca found her dead on the floor in her studio, we

both considered that our lucky break. We could stay and be Salvatores. No more moving around, no more abuse from my grandfather. At one point, I thought Damian had killed her until Arlo had her blood tested. A drug produced by Wellington Pharmaceuticals was in her bloodstream.

From that day forward, Arlo put all his time and energy into the four of us. We were his top priority. He was cruel and punished us, but he taught us everything we knew.

How to be men.

How to kill.

How to hunt.

He showed us how to make money, how to build real wealth. We learned how to intimidate people so we could maintain our power.

We became Salvatores.

No one ever treated us like we didn't belong with Arlo and his sons. The five of us clicked from day one. We were all alike in different ways, hardened by the world's cruelty. While Arlo grieved his late wife, he toughened us up and showed us the importance of securing our legacies.

I pulled up to the gate and hit a button on the call box. A man's voice blared through the speaker, and I gave him my name. The gate buzzed, then moved inward, so I could drive onto the property.

I swallowed hard, clearing the lump at the back of my throat. We couldn't bring our brothers with us. And we definitely couldn't let Alex tag along for the ride. My grandfather was cautious and calculated, planning every moment of his life down to the second. Bringing our entire family to The Hamptons without an invitation would have raised red flags.

I brought bullshit paperwork for Atlantic Airlines with me. Documents Luca had The Serpents forge to make them look like the real thing. That was their specialty. The Serpents could make anything fake look real. Everything from famous paintings and works of art to bank checks.

145

The documents would get us in the door without a guard putting a bullet in our skulls. My grandfather would undoubtedly be on high alert after his plan fell through. We still didn't know what he wanted from Carl Wellington's black book. He must have dirt on him even his money couldn't erase.

I parked in the circular driveway and tapped Damian on the shoulder. "D, you gotta get your head in the game. I can't do this without you."

He shifted in the seat and stared through me.

"Say something."

"I'm good," he muttered and then opened his door.

Damian was more traumatized by our one-month stay than me. I was too busy trying to console him to worry about myself. For most of my life, I felt like his keeper. Even my brothers relied on me to control Damian. Sometimes it was fucking exhausting. Like I had a grown child.

As we walked toward the house, the front doors swung open. My grandfather was nearing his eightieth birthday and still looked like he was in his late fifties.

When I was a kid, I wondered if he was a warlock or had magic because he never seemed to age. And then I realized he was pure fucking evil. The Devil incarnate. He never seemed human to me, like he wasn't even from this world.

"Fitzy," I said as I passed by the guards, mentally preparing myself for a battle. "You look well."

He didn't like being called grandfather or any variation of the name because it made him feel old.

The old man smirked as our eyes met. "And you look tired. Busy running after the Wellington girl, I see." He shook his head, disgust scrolling across his face. "Carl is weak for not putting a stop to that."

He'd already voiced his opinion about my relationship with Alex. People his age couldn't wrap their heads around a polyamorous relationship, especially one that involved my brothers. I couldn't blame him. It wasn't something I had considered until Alex entered our lives.

Luca hated her too much to touch her, let alone marry her. So he tasked Damian and me with tormenting her, all because he couldn't get over his anger. None of us would have ever gotten involved if he hadn't hated her so much. We would have let him have her.

His initial loss was our gain.

"Busy with Atlantic Airlines," I shot back, ignoring his statement about Alex.

She was none of his business.

He tipped his head at the folder in my hand. "Is that for me?"

I nodded.

His gaze drifted to Damian. He eyed him with the same evil glint in his eyes like the first time we walked into his home. Damian refused to look him directly in the eyes. Fitzy was the only person who had ever gotten under his skin.

He surveyed Damian for a few more seconds, then spun on his heels. "Come with me."

We walked in complete silence down the long marble hallway, decorated with various works of art from the Renaissance. Alex would have loved his collection. She was obsessed with da Vinci, Raphael, Botticelli, and all the greats. This house looked like a museum, with its white walls and floors and expensive but tasteful art. Most of the guards on the property were here to protect the rare collectibles.

We had accounted for the guards before we arrived. Marcello cut the live feeds and replaced them with a static image that would loop until we were off the estate.

Once inside his office on the second floor, I sat beside Damian on a worn leather couch. The room looked like a saloon from a Western movie. A long wooden bar stretched across the right side of the space. The furniture was old and smelled of cigars. He even had dead animal heads mounted in various places on the walls, with the largest one hanging over the fireplace.

I hated this house.

Hated this room.

And I hated him.

Just being in this room turned my stomach. Damian shifted awkwardly beside me, his thigh brushing mine. I wanted to put my hand on his knee to calm him down. But I knew my grandfather would see that as a weakness.

He thought we were both weak, even though we'd proved him otherwise over the years. In his eyes, we would always be the scared little boys sent to live with him.

I handed my grandfather the folder.

He took it with a smirk tipping up the right corner of his mouth. "Drink?"

"Sure."

He tilted his head to the bar. "I'll have a Macallan neat."

I wanted to choke the smug bastard to death. Teeth gritted, I rose from the couch while he flipped through the pages in the folder. The documentation looked legit. The three of us would sign on the dotted lines and celebrate the transaction, and then it was time for the next part of our plan.

After my grandfather learned about my relationship with Alex, he tried to strong-arm Damian and me into giving him a more significant percentage of Atlantic Airlines.

We both refused.

I stopped taking his calls, but he controlled most of our board members and threatened to have me removed as CEO. One of the many downfalls of running a publicly-traded company.

Fitzy owned a minority stake in Atlantic Airlines. My mother used a portion of her trust fund to bankroll the first few years of operating costs. So he demanded he gets his fair share.

I poured our drinks and handed a glass to Damian. He

swallowed the contents in one gulp and slammed the glass on the table.

That caught Fitzy's attention.

His head snapped to Damian, and his eyes narrowed. My brother gave him a challenging look that said, I dare you to say something, motherfucker.

I thought my grandfather would say some smart-ass shit to piss Damian off, but he was too pleased with the shareholder paperwork to fuck with him.

The prick thought he won.

He stuffed the signed papers in the folder and set his drink on top. "I think we're done here, boys."

"Not quite." I gulped down half of the scotch and resumed my place beside Damian. "We have something else to discuss." Then, leaning forward, I took another sip. "We know you hired Savanna Wellington to kidnap Alex."

His mouth snapped shut, and then his expression turned to stone.

"Don't deny it," I added with venom in my tone. "That bitch wouldn't stop flapping her jaw. She told us every single detail of your plan. Including the fact you wanted to sell Alex to Lorenzo Basile to get Carl Wellington's black book."

He snickered at my last comment.

"What do you have to hide?" I squeezed the glass in my hand. "What does Wellington have on you? What are you afraid of getting out?"

"Fine," he hissed. "You want to know the truth?" He downed the last of his scotch and shot up from the couch to pour another glass. "I hired Savanna to take the girl."

Anger seething through me, I followed him over to the bar. "Why?"

"For the book." He fixed himself a drink and spun around. "Carl is holding something over my head."

Crossing my arms over my chest, I leaned my back against

149

the bar. "You could have gotten Alex killed. And for what? A fucking book?"

"It's not just a book," he snapped. "You don't know the secrets Wellington has on us."

"On me?"

"All of us," he fired back. "Wellington has been trying to take my throne for years." He sipped from the highball glass. "It is your birthright to one day be an Elder. You are an Adams. That name means something. And Wellington is threatening to take it from us."

"Luca is marrying Alex. If we'd known you would kidnap and sell her to a Mafia boss, we would have given it to you." I got so close to him that our mouths were inches apart. "Why did you do it, old man?"

"Get out of my face." He shoved my chest with his palm. "How dare you disrespect me in my home?"

Damian was now at my side, breathing loudly through his nose. He looked like a fucking dragon about to spit fire. "Don't listen to him, Bash. He's a liar. Wellington isn't trying to take shit from him."

"You have no idea what you're talking about," Fitzy hissed at Damian. "And how could you possibly understand? Your father was a spineless, arrogant piece of shit." He sneered at him. "You may call yourself a Salvatore now, but you will always be Damian Townsend. The biological son of a conman, and the adopted son of a criminal."

Of all the things to say to Damian. He loved Arlo more than his bio dad. There wasn't anything he wouldn't have done for him. And with that, Damian wrapped his hands around Fitzy's throat, lifting his feet off the ground.

Damian slammed his back into the bar and then his head. "You hated my dad because he had the balls to stand up to you."

"He was nothing!" My grandfather gasped for air, reaching into his pocket for his cell phone. "Just like you."

I ripped the phone from his hand. "No one is coming to save you."

"My security team is downstairs," he growled. "You won't leave the premises alive."

"Your security team is clueless, old man. Do you think we would come here without a plan?"

Damian bashed his skull into the wood again. I had to pull Damian off my grandfather. We couldn't kill him, not like this.

Even if we both wanted to rip him limb from limb, it had to look like he died of natural causes. That was the deal we struck with Carl Wellington when we met at our estate.

Carl would become the new Grand Master of The Founders Society if we could pull this off. They would finally grant the Salvatores standing within the organization. The marriage to Alex would only be a bonus. All of our problems would go away.

But first, I had to kill one of my few living relatives. It didn't matter to me. He never acted like my grandfather or treated me like his flesh and blood.

Damian pressed down on Fitzy's shoulders, pinning him to the bar. I grabbed a glass of scotch and emptied the contents of five capsules into the drink. It was the same drug used to murder Evangeline Franco.

Even the same dose.

Wellington Pharmaceuticals had taken the pills off the market because of the lethal side effects. It would look like Fitzy had a heart attack. An easy death for someone who deserved so much worse.

But what choice did we have?

We couldn't murder the wealthiest man in the world and then bury his body. He was on the boards of too many companies to go unnoticed, which would only draw suspicion back to my family. As his next of kin, I would have his ass cremated before anyone could challenge his death.

His eyes widened at the glass in my hand. "What are you doing with that?"

I moved it closer to his mouth. "You're going to drink it."

He swatted at my hand. "The two of you think you're so smart." Even with his imminent death rapidly approaching, he still didn't back down. "You have been chasing ghosts for years."

Damian tightened his grip on my grandfather, using his body to hold him down, so I could pry open his lips and pour the glass' contents into his mouth.

I forced the drug cocktail down his throat and covered his mouth with my hand. "This is for Alex," I told him. "And for the years you treated us like shit. Like we didn't matter. For everything you would have done to our family if you lived."

He tried to spit at me when I moved my hand but drooled on himself. "The Lucaya Group didn't kill your parents!"

I leaned over him. "Then who killed them?"

He groaned as the pills worked their way through his bloodstream. His eyelids fluttered and then closed.

I tapped Damian on the shoulder. "Let him go."

My grandfather's lips parted, struggling to get out the words. His hand flew to his heart, and as the bastard took his last breath, he said, "I had them killed."

Chapter Twenty-Seven

ALEX

All of us were on the edge of our seats, waiting for Damian and Bastian to return. So Luca opened a new bottle of Macallan and turned on the music. Marcello joined us in the sitting room after he disabled the security system at Fitzy's house.

It was all part of the plan.

Bastian had been texting with Luca, giving him periodic updates until a few hours ago. Then all communication ceased. They had turned off their cell phones, so Marcello couldn't even track them.

I couldn't drink, so I busied my mind by dancing for my men.

Luca gripped the backs of my thighs. "Dance for me."

"I thought I was."

He patted his leg with a sinful look in his pretty blue eyes. "Get up here and dance on my cock, baby girl."

I climbed on top of him and straddled his thighs. Luca pulled down the top of my dress. Marcello scooted across the leather sofa and grabbed my other breast. My eyes slammed shut when Marcello's mouth closed over my nipple, sucking and biting so hard I squealed. He looked up at me with the tiny bud between his teeth. I shoved my hands through his black hair and moaned as he nibbled on my skin.

Luca's hand moved between my thighs. "Do you need to come again, baby?"

I licked my lips and nodded.

With each flick of Marcello's tongue, I soaked right through my panties. Then, Luca pushed his finger inside me over the fabric. The friction drove me insane, especially with the two working together to make me come.

Luca inched his hand up my throat, his fingers branding my skin. He tightened his grip and brought my lips to his, invading my mouth with savage hunger.

I pushed my dress up my thighs, and he plunged two fingers inside me. "Luca," I whimpered, "Marcello."

While Marcello bit my sore nipple, I thrust my hips into Luca's hand, greedy and begging for more. I leaned forward and clutched their shoulders to steady myself as my skin heated from the inferno brewing within.

"That's it, baby," Luca growled, his blue eyes wild with desire. "Come for us. Squeeze my fingers like they're my cock."

"I want both of you," I moaned as my orgasm rolled over me in waves, spilling out of me like water breaking through a dam.

Luca sucked my lip into his mouth. "Take off your dress." His hands moved to my ass, and he squeezed. "I need to touch you. Feel you. Taste you. Fuck you."

I rubbed my pussy on his cock. "Unzip me."

He reached behind me and tugged on the zipper. His blue eyes flickered with complete and total madness as I peeled the fabric from my body. When the song switched to an upbeat rap, I shook my breasts in his face, dancing on top of him.

Marcello got off the couch and moved behind me, gathering my hair in his hands. He slid the hair off my shoulder and licked my skin. I loved when he was playful but still a hunter like his brothers.

He cupped my breasts and rolled the pads of his thumbs over my painfully sore nipples. "I need to fuck you, princess."

"Not yet," Luca ordered, always in control. He gripped my thighs and lifted my legs over his shoulder, pushing me backward so he could move his head between my legs. "Wait your turn, brother."

"Fuck you," Marcello challenged.

Luca rolled his eyes, and seconds later, his lips were on my skin, kissing and nibbling his way to my throbbing core. He removed a knife from inside his jacket pocket. My heart caught in my throat as his eyes met mine. My sexy devil sliced the thin lace, tearing my panties clean off my body, and discarded them as if they were nothing.

He dropped the knife onto the couch and sucked on my clit, slamming his fingers into my wetness. My eyes snapped shut when he added another finger, rough and ruthless, taking what he wanted from me. As I hooked my legs around his neck, I leaned back on Marcello. He dipped his head down and parted my lips with his tongue, devouring me. Between the two of them, my entire body was on fire.

Luca removed his fingers from my pussy and ate me like a starved man. Deeper and deeper, his tongue left no part of me uncharted.

"Luca," I moaned as Marcello massaged my nipples. "Oh, my God. Mmm… I'm going to come."

"Good girl," Marcello growled against my neck.

Sweat slid between my breasts as my body trembled, chasing one orgasm and then another as they poured out of me in waves. My heart hammered in my chest as the last tremor rocked through me. Luca slid my legs off his shoulders and wrapped them around his back so I was straddling him.

I sat up and grabbed his tie, pulling his lips to mine. Our tongues tangled together, and I could taste myself on him as we kissed. I ripped off his tie and began working on the buttons of his dress shirt. He shoved the suit jacket over his shoulders, and his shirt was next. Luca pushed down his pants and boxers, and I helped him discard them.

I stared into his eyes and waited for him to make the next move. His hand fell to the back of my head, giving me a gentle push. So I got on my knees before him.

"Be a good girl," he groaned as his fingers wove through my hair. "Suck my cock."

"Marcello." I glanced over my shoulder. "Take off your clothes. Fuck me."

He didn't waste a second, and Luca didn't complain. Unlike his brothers, he didn't like sharing me. But as Marcello stripped and bent me over Luca's lap, he didn't say a word. Luca clutched my curls and shoved my mouth onto his cock as Marcello broke through my inner walls.

Wrapping my hand around Luca, I pumped him into my mouth, taking him inch by inch until I could feel him in the back of my throat. His groans turned feral as I hummed on his big dick while his brother fucked me without mercy.

Marcello gripped my hips, slamming in and out of me as if he would never get to fuck me again. My protective prince was usually the sweet one. He never made waves and always treated me like I was breakable. But whenever we were both around Luca, he got more possessive of me.

More aggressive.

Tears leaked from my eyes and streamed down my cheeks. Luca noticed I couldn't handle all of him and popped out of my mouth.

He swiped his thumbs across my cheeks to wipe away the tears. "She's pregnant, asshole," Luca snapped at Marcello. "Calm the fuck down."

After Marcello came inside me, he completely stilled. His fingers slid beneath my chin, and he tilted my head back until our eyes met. "Are you okay, princess? Did I fuck you too hard?"

I shook my head. "No. It felt good."

He wiped the sweat from his forehead and groaned. "Are you sure?"

"Yes, I'm sure."

Annoyed with him, Luca shoved him to the side and lifted me onto his lap. He drove into me. His cock was so deep inside me he could have left an imprint. Marcello played with my nipples while Luca bounced me up and down on his cock. It felt so good to be loved and worshiped by both of them.

I loved seeing Luca so protective over me. Even though I didn't need him to yell at Marcello mid-sex for being too rough. It wasn't the first time I almost choked on one of them.

Another orgasm stirred inside me. Heat spread down my chest, arms, and thighs. I clutched Luca's shoulders and kissed him as my entire body trembled, hitting the peak of my climax. And then Luca was right after me, losing himself.

"My Queen D." Luca gave my ass a light tap. "You're delicious."

Before I collapsed, he hooked his arm around my middle and sat me beside him on the couch. Drenched in sweat, Marcello plopped down beside us, naked and looking so fucking sexy. His hand rested on my knee. I was a little tired, a common theme lately, but I still wanted more.

The front door slammed.

All three of us shot up from the couch. We didn't bother to put on clothes and walked into the hallway.

Luca moved in front of us, hands on his hips, as his brothers strolled down the corridor toward us. "So? What did he say?"

Bastian and Damian stared at us as if they weren't in their bodies. It wasn't the same as when Damian went to his dark place. There wasn't the same crazed look in his green eyes. It was like no one was home, chilling me to the bone.

Bastian blinked a few times in rapid succession while Damian looked through me. How the hell did they drive from The Hamptons in this condition?

I stepped forward and waved my hand in front of Bastian's face. "Hey, talk to us." His eyes lowered at me. "Bash, what happened?"

"He's dead," he muttered.

When I looked into his eyes, they were glassy and red around the rim. Like he had been crying.

I inched my fingers up his arm. "Are you okay?"

He shook his head.

"What fucking happened?" Luca's deep voice echoed off the high ceiling. "What did he say?"

"He killed our parents." Bastian latched onto Damian, dragging him in the opposite direction.

My mouth dropped at his confession. Even Luca and Marcello looked equally surprised.

"Where are you going?" I asked them.

"We need to be alone," Bastian said without looking back at me.

As they climbed the staircase to the second floor, Luca muttered, "That explains a lot." Then, he moved forward as if he were about to go after them.

I clamped my fingers around his wrist. "Let them go. Give them the night to deal with this on their own."

"But we need to know what Fitzy said to them," he pointed out. "Our lives could be in danger."

I shook my head. "Did you see them? They're not okay. And if they thought our lives were in danger, they would have warned us. So let them have some time to process."

My heart ached for both of them. I wanted to run upstairs and throw myself into their arms. Tell them everything would be okay. But it was clear they needed to be together, with none of us getting in the way.

Not even me.

Chapter Twenty-Eight

BASTIAN

We sat on my bed and didn't speak. Damian was a man of few words, so it suited us just fine. But I couldn't sit still and needed to vent my frustrations.

Damian moved his hand to my knee to stop me from shaking. I turned my head to look into his glassy green eyes.

"It's over, D," I said to break the silence. "We waited years to get revenge. So why doesn't it feel the way I thought it would?"

His lips thinned into a straight line. He hadn't spoken more than a few sentences since we got into my car and drove to The Hamptons. Even after Fitzy's heart stopped beating, he just stood there, staring at the old man.

I called a guard into the room. He didn't suspect us of wrongdoing and handled everything according to my grandfather's request. He had a death plan, which we carried out perfectly.

"He led us to believe The Lucaya Group killed our parents," I muttered. "Why? I still don't get it."

"It was easier to blame a known terrorist organization than admit what he'd done."

"He killed his daughter." A single tear slid down my cheek. "He fucking killed our parents to drive down the stock price."

It was always about the money with my grandfather. He was the wealthiest man in the world, and now I understood how he had amassed so much wealth.

"He hated my dad." Damian squeezed my knee for support. "Yours too. Maybe he didn't know our moms would be on the flight."

"They were supposed to be at my recital," I whispered.

Like a dam breaking, the tears flowed out of me, my entire body shaking. I rested my head on Damian's shoulder and cried like a baby, letting out everything I'd held in for the past fifteen years. Fitzy punished us when we cried about our parents. He locked us in his basement and turned out the lights.

We learned that feelings got us in trouble. So we shut them out, pretended we didn't feel anymore. Then, after a while, we stopped feeling anything, not even our pain.

"He wouldn't kill his daughter, right?" I lifted my head from his shoulder, tears streaming down my cheeks. "I just can't... I don't understand."

Damian swiped the pad of his thumb beneath my eyes. "She defied him. Spent two-thirds of her trust fund to start Atlantic Airlines. He never supported her decision. And he also never accepted your parents' marriage. I wouldn't put anything past the old man."

I threw my arms around him, needing a fucking hug. "You're the only person who understands, D. I wouldn't have made it through all this shit without you."

He hugged me back. "You've always taken care of me." Then he tilted my chin until our eyes met. "Let me take care of you, Bash."

I loved Alex. But with Damian, nothing was black or white. We mainly lived in the gray area. So when he grabbed the side of my face, and his tongue swept into my mouth, I didn't push him away. Instead, I gripped his shirt and kissed him back.

Alex had unlocked the soft, caring, loving part of Damian. He was like that until we were eight years old.

After he saw his dad cheating on his mom with his babysitter, a girl closer to his age than his dad, he changed. Later that day, he went back and snapped a bird's neck. Said it was to end its suffering. But I never believed that story.

Didn't matter, anyway.

Because I loved him unconditionally. Never judged him, not once in our lives. Even when I disagreed with his choices, I never made him feel bad for having dark desires.

So I let him push my chest and climb on top of me. In the bedroom, I was always the aggressor. But with Damian, it was a push-pull, the two of us fighting for control over the other. I didn't give a fuck tonight, not after killing my grandfather. Not after he admitted to murdering our parents.

I just wanted to feel.

Something.

Anything.

And I wanted to feel it with the one person who felt the same anger, sadness, and emptiness. I felt like someone had punched a hole through my chest, ripped out my heart, and squeezed so hard it turned to dust.

I felt nothing.

And everything.

His tongue was in my mouth, his hands all over my skin. I pushed his head lower, and he unzipped my pants and shoved them down with my boxers. My cock was so fucking hard, pre-cum sliding down the tip.

He wrapped his hand around my shaft and stroked me so hard my eyes slammed shut. I could hardly catch my breath, panting for more. There was something about when Damian touched me that was unlike women.

Even different from Alex.

When I opened my eyes, he licked the head of my cock, and my skin crackled with electricity. Every nerve ending in my body set on fire as he sucked me into his mouth.

I'd gotten my first blowjob from Damian. A fact I didn't broadcast. Back then, I was so fucked up over what we did that I begged my dad to take me to The Mansion. I needed to prove to myself I didn't like men. So I fucked as many women as I could, buried myself so deep inside them I forgot about loving the feel of my cock in his mouth.

Damian never gave a damn.

He knew he wasn't gay and never challenged his sexuality. But I couldn't wrap my head around how I felt about him. My feelings were specific to Damian. No other man had ever gotten me hard.

And as he pumped my cock into his mouth, I moved my hand to the back of his head. "Fuck," I groaned, forcing him to take more, my chest heaving with each breath.

I fisted his short black hair, and his green eyes found mine. I no longer cared about what people thought about us. Everyone in the house knew we had our moments.

My legs trembled, an orgasm brewing inside me. Damian grabbed my thigh and held me down, moving his other hand between my legs. He pressed his finger at the entrance to my ass, and when I didn't stop him, he pushed it inside me. Biting down on my bottom lip, I closed my eyes and breathed through my nose.

I wanted to feel the pain.

I wanted to feel something.

After a few more times, my body adjusted to the change, and I relaxed as he sucked my cock, working his finger into my ass. Damian tried to fuck me dozens of times, especially when he was high from the bloodlust. He would pin me down and choke me from behind, but I wouldn't let him take it any farther.

A few times, he'd even begged me to fuck him. I couldn't

go through with it, not even when I knew he needed it. Not even when he was out of his mind.

But I no longer felt the same shame.

"Fuck, D." I put both hands on the back of his head, forcing him to take more of me right as I hit the peak of my climax.

I came hard on his tongue, filling his mouth with my cum. He sat up and wiped his lips with the back of his hand, staring at me like a hunter as he undressed.

I knew what he wanted.

And I wanted it, too.

So I reached for my phone on the nightstand and texted Alex, asking her to come to my room.

A minute later, she entered my bedroom, still naked, her big tits shaking as she walked toward us. I could see her stomach growing, though it wouldn't be noticeable to most people.

"We don't want to talk," I told her.

A smile tipped up her mouth. "Good. Because I'd rather fuck." She stopped in front of the bed, her eyes shifting between us. "Have you two been playing without me?"

"If I say yes, will you be mad?"

She shook her head, rubbing her nipples with the pads of her thumbs. "The thought of you guys together turns me on."

I reached out and hooked my arm around her, pulling her onto the mattress. "I let Damian finger my ass while he sucked my cock."

"Mmm... What else did you do?" She laid back on my chest, her thighs spread. Damian moved between them, leaning on his elbows as he circled her clit with his thumb. "Oh, my God, Damian."

"Nothing yet," I confessed. "That's why I texted."

She moaned, her eyes rolling into the back of her head as Damian quickened his pace. "Can I watch?"

I slid the curls out of her eyes and twisted her nipple,

ripping a scream from her pretty lips. "We don't want you to watch, Cherry."

Her eyebrow lifted as she looked up at me. "Should I leave?"

"Not a chance." I squeezed her tit. "Grab the lube from the drawer."

I took the bottle from her hand and shoved her onto the bed, ordering Damian to fuck her. He slammed his cock into our beautiful girl, and her screams of pleasure filled the silence in the room. Consumed by the sweet scent of her pussy, and the sounds she made for Damian, I was so fucking hard my cock twitched.

I coated my finger with lube and put my other hand on Damian's lower back. He slowed his pace for a second, long enough for me to plunge my finger into his ass. I couldn't believe I was going to do this. I fought him for years, and after tonight, I didn't care anymore.

Didn't care about anything.

I wasn't even sure who I thought I would disappoint by fucking a man. My brothers didn't care. Alex was down for anything and encouraged us to explore our feelings.

Damian grunted when I replaced my finger with my cock, slowly inching inside him. He was so tight. But fuck, it felt so damn good.

Leaning over Alex, he put his hands on each side of her on the mattress. She looked up at us, and her lips parted, her eyes wild with desire. I love you, she mouthed as she held my gaze.

I said it back.

Once Damian's body relaxed, we worked as a team, our bodies moving in unison.

He felt good.

Given the circumstances of the night, it felt right. Maybe that was why I'd never given in to the temptation before. I needed to shed the parts of myself that belonged to someone else, the broken, damaged pieces that died tonight.

I grabbed Damian's shoulder and pressed my chest to his back. Sweat coated my skin, sliding down my forehead and stomach. Dragging my teeth across his neck, I thrust into him harder, loving the feel of him, high from Alex's screams and Damian's groans.

He wrapped my fingers around his throat, and I squeezed just the way he liked it. Then, we came one after the other and collapsed on the bed.

With Alex between us, a hand on her chest, she stared at the ceiling. "Wow! That was hot."

Damian breathed hard, too stunned to speak.

I rolled onto my side and squeezed her breast. "Your tits are getting huge." I lowered my head and sucked her nipple into my mouth. "Are you still sore, baby?"

"It comes and goes." She expelled the air from her lungs, still trying to catch her breath. "I'm just glad the morning sickness is gone. That was a nightmare."

"You're having Damian's baby," I pointed out. "It's probably possessed. So we may need a priest on standby when you give birth to perform an exorcism."

Alex laughed.

Damian reached over and smacked the side of my head. "You're just jealous the baby is mine."

I rubbed my hand over her stomach. "I don't care whose baby you're having. We're in this together, all five of us. This baby is mine, too."

Alex grabbed Damian's hand and covered it with mine. "I love both of you. So will this baby. She's lucky to have you."

"We don't know the sex."

She looked at me with a big smile on her pretty face. "I have dreams about a little girl with long black hair."

"Maybe you're manifesting her," I quipped.

She shook her head and smiled. "I can feel it. Call it intuition. But I think I'm having a girl." Alex turned her head to the side to look at Damian. "How do you feel about having a girl?"

"Scared," he admitted. "I don't know how to take care of a baby."

"You take care of me," she cooed.

"No, I don't." He laughed at the idea. "My brothers handle everything because they don't think I can do it."

"That's not why," I fired back. "Luca has to control her schedule and her wardrobe. Marcello enjoys being her bodyguard." I bent down and kissed her forehead. "And I make sure she knows we love her."

"What am I supposed to do?" Damian bit the inside of his cheek. "What's left?"

Alex clutched his hand. "Take care of the baby and me. That's your job now."

"How?"

His question sounded strange, but it was valid to him. I could see him asking Dr. Langston the same question. Damian often asked questions normal people could answer without a second thought.

"You can start by sleeping with me."

He curled his arm around her and pulled her closer. "We have to sleep with Bash." He glanced over at me. "Just in case."

"The nightmares," Alex commented.

He nodded. "I don't want to hurt you or the baby in my sleep."

"This is a start." A grin tugged at her mouth. "When I say take care of us, I want you to be here. Don't run from me. No more hiding when you can't deal."

"I can do that," he said in a hushed tone.

Alex moved his hand between her legs and shoved his fingers inside her. "Right now, I need you to take care of me."

A genuine smile that touched his eyes lit his face as he

climbed on top of her. I kissed our girl, and she moaned into my mouth. Damian made love to her, soft and slow. For years, he thought he wasn't capable of anything other than violence. But the past few months had proved otherwise.

I kissed Alex. Then I grabbed the back of Damian's head and kissed him, too. Alex wrapped her hand around my cock, her strokes matching Damian's thrusts.

We kissed and fucked, forgetting about the day's events, and focused on our future. The old Bastian died tonight, replaced by someone new. And after we collapsed onto the mattress together, I noticed the change in Damian, too.

Chapter Twenty-Nine

LUCA

O ver breakfast, Bastian and Damian filled us in on Fitzy's betrayal. Carl had discovered his secret right before Alex's kidnapping. I still didn't trust Wellington. But after I married Alex, I would be privy to his secrets, which brought me some comfort.

Later in the day, I found Alex in my mother's studio. She sat on the floor and dipped her brush into the gold paint. It was like she was allergic to painting in a chair. Most of the time, she lifted the canvas off the easel and laid it on a tarp.

Alex looked up from the canvas when I stopped in front of her. "Is something wrong?"

I shook my head. "Can't a man stare at his wife without something being wrong?"

She twirled a paintbrush between her fingers and chuckled. "I thought you were busy organizing the ceremony."

I dropped to the floor beside her on one knee. "Legare is tomorrow night. You'll be forever bound to the four of us." She smiled at that, and I extended my hand. "There's something I want to show you. It's a surprise."

Alex placed her hand in mine, and I helped her up from the floor. "Do I get a hint?"

"Nope."

I led her across the room with my hand on her lower back.

"You're making me nervous," she muttered.

"This is a good surprise, baby. You have nothing to worry about."

We climbed the stairs to the fourth floor. Marcello and my father had rooms at opposite ends. I had saved one room for Alex a long time ago, waiting until the day she became my wife.

At the end of the hallway, I stopped before a set of double doors and handed Alex a skeleton key. This was an old house built back in the early 1900s.

I dangled the gold key from a silky red string.

Alex's eyes widened as she grabbed it. "What's inside?"

I tipped my head at the doors. "See for yourself."

Apprehensive, she shoved the key into the lock. I hit the light switch on the wall, and Alex gasped.

Her hand flew to her mouth. "Oh, my God, Luca." She spoke between her fingers. "You did this for me?"

I guided her into the room by her hip. "Everything I do is for you. Don't you know that by now?"

Her eyes darted around the expanse of the room. It was a replica of my mother's studio with hardwood floors and the same domed ceiling. Except this one was free of my mother's influence. The studio belonged to Alex. Every painting in the Many Faces of the Devil series hung on the walls. Framed photos of Alex from every art school exhibition. And with the help of her brother, I had all her sketches.

"How did you get these?" Her mouth widened as she looked at me. "You weren't even at my showcases at RISD."

I smirked. "I have my ways."

She shook her head in disbelief. "I'm speechless, Luca. This is incredible."

"You can paint a fresco." I waved my hand around the room. "The walls and ceiling are your canvas."

Her eyes watered as she looked at me.

Then she strolled across the room and stopped in front of the paintings from her final year at the Rhode Island School of Design. "How did you get these? I gave them to the school."

"I made a sizable donation."

She wiped away her happy tears and sighed. "You are such a psycho, Luca."

I hooked my arm around her, breathing in the scent of her delicious perfume. "A psycho in love is more dangerous than a man in love. Remember that the next time you test me."

"No kidding," she quipped. "I wish I could say I'm surprised you went to such lengths, but I always knew you were never far. I could always sense your presence, even when we were apart."

"I have everything you ever painted." I pointed at the drawings on the wall. "Even the sketches you threw out."

Her mouth widened. "You went through my trash?"

"There was never a time I didn't have someone watch over you. You are too important to me." I motioned toward the framed papers on the wall. "I asked your brother to make a collage of your scrapped designs. I thought maybe one day you could use them as inspiration."

She laughed. "You're anything but predictable, Luca."

"Do you like your new studio?"

The corners of her mouth turned up into a smile. "No, I love it."

I slipped my fingers through her curls. "This room is yours to do with as you wish. You shouldn't have to live in the shadow of my mother. This house is yours, too. Whatever you want, it's yours."

She threw her arms around my neck and kissed my lips. "I love you so much, you crazy lunatic. Thank you, Luca. Thank you for protecting me, even when I didn't know I needed your protection. For loving me."

"There is no line I wouldn't cross for you."

"I love it," she whispered. "This is the best gift you've ever given me."

When our lips separated, I looked into Alex's eyes, brushing her hair behind her ear.

"I want to paint all four of you in my new studio."

I raised her hand to my mouth and kissed her skin. "As you wish, my queen."

Chapter Thirty

ALEX

With death comes life, and with sadness comes joy. I told myself that as I stared at my changing body in the mirror. The weight gain was subtle but enough for me to notice.

My men were afraid to waste another second, especially now that Fitzy was dead. So we needed to move forward with Legare, the ceremony that would crown me Queen of The Devil's Knights, binding me to my men forever.

My grandfather was transitioning into his new role as the Grand Master of The Founders Society, but until it was official, we were still on edge. Only a few days had passed since Fitzy's funeral. Bastian and Damian seemed to bounce back quickly, leaving their pain and the past behind them. They shed those parts of themselves the night we shared our bodies.

Luca entered my bedroom, quiet as a mouse, and moved behind me. His blue eyes met mine in the mirror as I fixed the silky white gown. The paper-thin ceremonial dress barely covered my breasts. Not like it mattered since you could see my nipples through the fabric. A slit ran up the length of my thigh. I wasn't wearing panties because what was the point? We would undress in front of The Devil's Knights.

Nerves shook through me. Luca pressed his warm body against my back, and I felt safe, comforted by his touch. He always seemed to know when I needed him.

"Don't be afraid, *mi amore*," he whispered. "The Knights will do anything for their queen. This isn't about sex. It's about them pledging their loyalty."

I spun around to face him and kissed his lips. "It's important I'm bound to all four of you."

"You will be soon." His tongue swept into my mouth with a fiery passion, which only made me crave more of him as our lips separated. "Are you ready, Mrs. Salvatore?"

Yesterday, we went down to the courthouse and made it official. We didn't want to leave anything to chance with Lorenzo on the loose. The wedding our families had planned was only for show, an attempt to lure Lorenzo out of hiding. We assumed he would try to break up the wedding so he could steal me away from his nephews.

Besides, Legare was the actual binding of the five of us. Tonight, my men would become mine in every way that mattered. I couldn't just marry one, not when all of them were mine. So in our minds, this was our wedding and even more important.

I offered Luca my hand and smiled.

"Mrs. Salvatore," he said with a grin. "I've been waiting a long time to call you that."

He led me downstairs, where his brothers waited in the sitting room with Sonny, Drake, Callum, Finn, and Cole. As part of the ritual, the sons of the founding families of Devil's Creek had to witness our union.

They stopped talking when we walked into the room. All of their eyes drifted up and down the length of my body, stripping me bare.

"Let's go," Luca ordered. "It's time."

He led me out of the sitting room and headed toward the front door. Everyone trailed behind in silence. I could hear my heart pounding as we approached the limousine waiting for us. We piled inside without a word, the silence in the air hanging between us as we drove off the estate.

"All of this uncomfortable silence is freaking me out," I told them. "Someone, please turn on music or say something."

Luca ordered Sonny to deal with distributing the alcohol. A rap beat floated through the air, ridding us of the awkward silence. My other three guys sat across from us, watching me with desire on their handsome faces. I couldn't wait to touch them, to be bound to them more permanently.

Luca pulled me onto his lap with one hand on my breast and the other between my legs. "Already making my cock hard," he groaned. "Wait until we get to the temple."

To torture him, I rubbed my ass on his erection. "Can't wait."

We arrived at the marina a few minutes later. Luca helped me out of the limo and slid his arm behind my back. My dress swept across the ground as we walked toward the bay. With my shoulders bare, my skin dotted with tiny bumps from the soft breeze blowing off the water. I felt like a Roman goddess in this dress, elegant and ethereal, in every way a queen.

We walked down a flight of stairs, past The Founders Club entrance, and into the catacombs beneath Devil's Creek. Salt and the scent of moss floated through the air. With each step we took underground, my nose twitched from my stupid allergies.

Luca removed a skeleton key from his pocket and pulled a brick from the wall. He inserted the key into a lock, and Marcello helped him open the hidden door.

We rounded one corner, then another, the space dimly lit by lanterns hung on the walls. Peculiar symbols etched into the stone walls lit by lanterns. I'd noticed a strange, demonic type of art the last time we were in the temple.

I pointed at the drawings as we passed. "What are those?"

"You know how the Freemasons have symbols?" Luca said. "We have our own."

"Don't the Masons work with their hands? I can't see many rich boys hanging out down here to carve symbols into the walls."

"I take offense at that," Sonny said with laughter in his tone.

"What?" I glanced over my shoulder at him. "When have any of you ever worked with your hands?"

"Please," Sonny shot back. "I'll show you how good I am with my hands."

"Stop flirting with my wife, Cormac," Luca growled.

We stopped in front of double doors with tons of symbols on them. Two thrones sat atop a dais at the far end of the room. At the center was a bed draped in black and red sheets.

Luca led me to our thrones and lifted a black robe from the back of his chair. The Knights headed to the right side, where they changed into similar black cloaks with hoods.

Luca pointed at the thrones. "Sit, my queen."

I did as he instructed, then he sat beside me with his hand on my thigh.

"How does this work?" I asked.

"I'll guide you every step of the way." Resting his elbow on the arm of the chair, he leaned over to speak in a hushed tone. "After we consummate our union, we will crown you queen."

I couldn't stop smiling.

"Does this make you happy?"

I nodded. "Never thought I'd get a coronation."

Luca winked. "You get more than a crown, baby."

After the Knights dressed in ceremonial robes, they stood a few feet from the dais.

Luca tapped my thigh and whispered, "Follow my lead."

I rose from the throne and stood at his side. His fingers brushed mine, so I took that as a sign he wanted me to hold his hand. We stopped in front of the Knights, dressed in black cloaks, their faces concealed by the hoods.

Luca had been tight-lipped about most of the ritual. He wanted me to experience everything with fresh eyes, with no expectations. But not knowing had only made me more nervous about how this night would unfold.

He moved in front of me, shoved my curls over my left shoulder, and stared at me with a rare smile. He looked so handsome when he smiled. But how often did he do that? Maybe a little more now that we were officially together.

Luca dropped to one knee in front of me. "My queen."

He raised my hand to his lips and kissed my skin, his eyes never leaving mine. A burst of heat rushed down my arm as Luca kissed my other hand.

It felt so good to be loved by him.

When he wasn't playing games and lowered his guard, there was nothing more beautiful than this man kneeling before me. Luca rose to his full height. Then he slipped his finger beneath the thin strap over my shoulder. The left side of the dress fell to my belly button. White and nearly see-through, I felt anything but pure in this dress.

I stared at Luca with my heart hammering out of my chest. He stripped away my gown. The fabric gathered around my feet, and I kicked it aside. Even though I couldn't see their faces, I could feel the Knights watching me with admiration.

Luca rubbed his thumb across my bottom lip before he turned to face them. "Knights, I present to you, Alexandrea Salvatore. Do you swear an oath to protect your queen, no matter the cost, from this day forth?"

"We swear an oath to you, Alexandrea Salvatore, our one true queen," the Knights said in unison.

Luca turned to me. "And do you, Alexandrea, promise to follow the laws that govern The Devil's Knights?"

I'd read most of the Charter the night before, but it was a

thick tome. With the help of my guys, I understood how the organization worked and felt confident in agreeing to their terms.

"Yes," I muttered.

"As our Queen, will you aid The Devil's Knights in carrying out the laws outlined in the Charter?"

"Yes."

Luca walked over to the table on our right and lifted a knife. He sliced the tip of his finger and let his blood drip into the basin. I moved to his side and grabbed the knife, repeating the process.

After I passed the blade to Marcello, and he cut into his skin, Bastian and Damian did the same.

"What binds us will destroy us," Luca said as his gaze moved between us.

His brothers chanted the words.

Luca looked at me to finish the ritual.

"What binds us will destroy us."

"And what will destroy us unites us," Luca said with his eyes on me.

This time, I said the words in unison with my husbands.

After we bound ourselves by blood, they circled me and then dropped to their knees. I stepped forward, and they lowered their hood-covered heads.

Luca moved behind me and gathered my curls in his hands, dipping his head down to kiss my neck. "What do you want, my queen?"

"You," I whispered.

Luca's fingers trailed down my hot skin, his sinful touch leaving fire in his wake. I leaned back against his chest, reveling in the pleasure of his lips on my neck, his tongue gliding across my skin. His long fingers brushed my right arm, and my skin pebbled with tiny bumps from his delicate touch. He continued his slow perusal of my body, and I moaned as his thumbs rolled over my nipples.

I let him touch me for a few seconds before shoving Marcello's hood off his head. He tilted his head back so I could stare into his sad blue eyes. With one look from my sexy prince, my heart leaped out of my chest.

His eyes raked over every inch of my naked body. I held out my hands, and he slipped his fingers between mine. Luca whispered the words I needed to say into my ear.

"I choose you, Marcello Salvatore. Do you swear to protect your queen, now and forever?"

Marcello nodded. "I do."

I moved his big hand to my inner thigh, and he looked at me for instructions. It was such a strange ritual. Alpha men like Marcello and the Knights didn't take orders from anyone, yet in this temple, they listened to me.

A thrill rushed down my arms as I guided his hand up my thigh. Marcello licked his lips, staring at me with desire in his eyes. Luca dug his fingers into my hips and resumed his gentle kisses along my neck and jaw.

Marcello knew what I wanted and took charge, gripping my thighs with both hands as he licked my clit. A flush of heat rushed through my body. My eyes snapped shut, and I moaned as Marcello's tongue slipped between my folds.

"Before we get carried away," Luca said against the shell of my ear, "you need to choose the next Knight."

I repeated the same process with Damian and Bastian. The other five Knights remained in place, their heads bowed. They weren't part of the ceremony, only here as witnesses.

Luca led me to the bed at the center of the room. His fingers burrowed into my hips, his rough touch branding my skin like hot pokers. He lifted me onto the bed and stood between my spread thighs. Damian, Marcello, and Bastian lined up behind him while the rest of the Knights watched us from a distance.

Taking the lead, Luca pressed his lips to mine, parting them with his tongue, kissing me with so much passion my head spun. Then, with a savage hunger, he devoured me with each flick of his tongue, marking me in front of our loyal subjects.

As our lips separated, I struggled to catch my breath, desperate for more of his skilled tongue. His eyes flickered with pure insanity, the usual madness brewing at the surface.

I gripped his robe in my hands. "Let's see how many times your brothers can make me come before you get jealous and have your way with me."

A low rumble escaped his throat. "I don't get jealous."

"Yes, you do." I gave him a quick kiss. "You share me with your brothers when you'd rather have me all to yourself."

He shook his head, and dark hair fell onto his forehead. "It turns me on watching you claim them."

I hooked my legs around his back and inched my hands up his chest. "I want you to claim me first."

Luca's fingers wove through my curls as he tilted my head to the side, his teeth grazing my hot skin, taking turns sucking and biting me. My handsome prince pinned me down with his hand on my stomach. Intense waves of pleasure rolled off my skin like flames.

When his head dipped between my legs, I rolled my head to the side to look at my men. Marcello wet his lips as he watched his brother lick my pussy. Bastian's eyes focused on me, his chest rising and falling with each breath. Damian ran a hand through his hair and licked his blood-red lips, giving me a heated look that made my skin sizzle with desire.

Luca worked his magic on my clit, sucked so hard my legs trembled, and I screamed his name. After coming down from my high, I beckoned Bastian with my index finger. He moved to the other side of the table from Luca and held down my arms. And then his lips were on mine, his tongue invading my mouth.

Luca made me come once more before I tugged on Bastian's robe. "Take off your clothes," I ordered, then looked at Luca and each of my guys. "Strip."

Luca gave me a wicked grin as he made of show of taking off his robe. The others didn't waste a second.

"How long do you think you'll last until you get jealous and need to be inside me?" I teased Luca with a sexy smile plastered on my face.

"I waited six years to fuck you." He clicked his tongue. "I can make it until the end of the ceremony."

"Guess we'll find out," I taunted. "We're done playing for now. Make room for my husbands."

"Bad girl," he said in a deep tone that rolled over me like a melody.

Then he stepped back, allowing Marcello and Damian to approach the table. Bastian massaged my breast, giving the tiny bud a pinch, stealing a scream from my throat. Marcello moved to my right, Damian on my left. With the three of them surrounding me, and the others watching us, I felt like a queen claiming her Knights.

I kissed my way down Bastian's muscular abdomen and gave his big dick a few strokes. Marcello and Damian each gripped one of my legs and spread them apart. As I leaned forward to suck Bastian into my mouth, Damian licked my pussy, his tongue sliding straight down the middle.

Marcello reached between us, and then two of his long fingers split me open. I was so wet my cum dripped onto his hand and the sheets.

Bastian tugged on my hair, practically choking me as his brothers made me come. My arms and legs shook uncontrollably, making it harder to hold myself up and maintain a steady rhythm. So Bastian gripped my shoulders and held me up, helping me steady myself as the orgasm ripped through me.

I grabbed Marcello's shoulders and kissed him. My loyal protector, my best friend, my one constant. His love for me poured out of him every time we were together. And as we kissed, he consumed me, drowning me in his love.

I breathed hard as our lips separated.

Before I could recover from our hot kiss, Marcello had me on my back, licking my pussy. Damian rubbed my clit with his thumb while Bastian wrapped his hand around my throat. It was light, just enough pressure to satisfy me. His lips were on mine again, and Damian was at his side, sucking my nipple into his mouth.

Consumed by all of their delicious scents, I drank them in, reveling in the feeling of their hands, tongues, and mouths on my body. After I came on Marcello's tongue a few times, Damian tapped his arm, gesturing for him to get out of the way. They had a system. None of them ever got mad when it wasn't their turn.

Damian flashed an evil grin before his tongue glided over my hot flesh. Bastian went back to rolling his thumb over my clit, while Marcello switched between massaging my breast and sucking on my nipple. I could feel each of them taking turns, fingers working in unison with Damian's tongue.

After all three of us came, Luca moved between my thighs. He tugged on my curls as his tongue swept into my mouth. Each kiss was rough and aggressive. Like he was shedding all his pent-up frustration over seeing me with his brothers.

Luca grabbed my throat, kissing me so hard and fast that I moaned into his mouth. He drove me wild, teasing me, taking his time until he finally filled me in one quick thrust. Heat coursed through my veins, warmth spreading down my arms and legs. I came once, twice, three times. He was wild and out of control, a man on a mission to mark his queen.

Claim his territory.

The Knights watched us from a distance. Even my guys didn't move from their places on the bed while Luca destroyed me. It felt like hours before Luca's body trembled, and his cock pulsed inside me. Out of breath, he crashed on top of me, his forehead and chest dripping with sweat.

Luca took my face in his hands and crushed my lips with a kiss. A ripple of emotions tore through my chest, rocking me to the core.

I loved him.

Married him.

Bound to all of them.

He helped me off the table and led me to the thrones at the front of the room. The Knights lined up in front of the dais.

Luca lifted a jeweled crown from a crimson pillow on the table beside him. My eyes widened at the magnificent piece. He moved in front of me, spoke a few words in Italian that I didn't understand, and then lowered the crown onto my head.

Long live the Queen of The Devil's Knights.

Chapter Thirty-One

ALEX

Everything was falling into place. I had the love of four incredible men, even though I still hadn't heard the words from Damian. He didn't need to say them. In his way, Damian loved his baby growing in my belly and me.

After years of having nothing and no one other than Aiden, I had a family that would do anything to protect me. A queen with Knights loyal to me for the rest of my life. Despite the lingering fear of Lorenzo showing up at the hotel, I told myself it would all be over soon. My guys had prepared for Lorenzo to seek his revenge. Our intel had shown him on his way to Connecticut last night.

Aiden stood behind me, his eyes meeting mine in the mirror. He brushed the hair off my shoulder and smiled. "You look beautiful, Lexie. Like the Black Swan."

That was the point.

Luca had seen the sketch but not the dress. I couldn't wait to see all of their faces when I walked down the aisle.

Charcoal lined my eyes, my cheeks pink from blush, and a light pink gloss on my lips. I rarely wore makeup, but since this was a special occasion, I told the makeup artist to go wild.

The second she saw the black feathers, her eyes widened, and she said my dress inspired the look.

He wrapped his arm around me. "I have to leave soon to finish my initiation."

"Can't you stay a little while longer?"

He shook his head. "I'm lucky the Knights let me stay this long. Luca only made the exception because of Lorenzo. After the wedding, I won't have any more excuses not to return to the safe house."

"What did they make you do?"

He turned his head away, unable to meet my gaze. "It's called a secret society for a reason."

"I'm the queen now," I reminded him.

"Every pledge class has different tasks they have to complete. I doubt my experience is the same as Luca and his brothers." His knuckles brushed my cheek. "I took a vow of secrecy. It could compromise other men in my class by telling you the details of my initiation."

"Don't tell me. I hope you're careful and not doing anything that will get you hurt, killed, or sent to prison."

He laughed. "Pops would never let that happen. Now that he controls The Founders Society, we're untouchable."

"That will be your legacy someday."

"No way," he shot back. "I already made a deal with Luca and Pops. After becoming a Knight, I will work with The Serpent Society. They need another forger."

I shook my head, unhappy with his decision, even though it made sense given his talents. My brother could imitate famous sculptors like Michelangelo and Bernini in his first year of college. He blew away his professors when he recreated a smaller version of Michelangelo's Bacchus.

"Does this mean you get to stay in Devil's Creek?" I asked him with a hopeful smile.

He nodded. "Three more months, and we'll never have to be apart again."

I rubbed my hand over my stomach. "You'll be an uncle soon. This baby will need you."

He touched my stomach, and a smile illuminated his handsome face. "Whatever you need, I'll be here."

The event planner popped her head into the room and announced it was time. Aiden held my hand as we followed her down the hallway. Because of the situation, Luca bought every room in the hotel. He even arranged for armed men and women to pose as hotel staff.

Luca had posted a wedding announcement in every newspaper and invited all the Mafia families. Everyone in the real world and the criminal underworld knew about the event. So we went into this with a plan and many allies who would have our backs. They had much more to gain from Lorenzo's death than any of us.

We stopped in front of the doors to the ballroom. The guests were already inside. I spotted Pops in a tuxedo beside my grandmonster. Blair stood ramrod straight, her posture so stiff I couldn't tell if she was breathing.

Since I didn't have bridesmaids, it sped up the timeline of the ceremony. I walked down the aisle with hundreds of eyes on me. You could easily spot the made men from the regular guests.

We stopped in front of Luca and the middle-aged man posing as the wedding officiate. Our marriage was already legal and binding. This was just a show for Lorenzo.

My brother dipped down to kiss my cheek and whispered to Luca that he better take care of me. Luca offered a smirk in response before Aiden took his place by my side. I had dreamed of my wedding day hundreds of times. And in all of those dreams, I always saw Luca next to me. Even when I hated him, I knew I would eventually marry him. He was part of me, etched into the very essence of my soul.

"You look beautiful, mi amore." Luca slipped his fingers between mine. "Like the queen of the underworld."

I smiled at his words, reminded of the diamond crown Luca sent to my dressing room an hour before the wedding, along with a drop diamond necklace and cuff bracelets. He made me feel like a queen in every way possible.

The officiate moved through the ceremony. And as we exchanged our wedding vows, I surprised Luca with a present. Before I slid the tungsten ring onto his finger, I turned it so he could see the inscription.

A genuine smile reached his blue eyes. "What binds us will destroy us."

Those words bound the five of us.

Even if I couldn't legally marry all of them, those words were the same as I do. So I got the same wedding band for each of them.

Luca lifted my hand to his lips, planting a soft kiss on my skin. Even in a room surrounded by people, I could only see the devilish prince from my dreams.

After the officiant pronounced us husband and wife, he hooked his arms around me and crushed my lips with a passionate kiss.

Our tongues tangled, fighting possession over the other as we lost ourselves. He held my chin like he was afraid I would disappear if he let go. Overcome by emotion, I kissed him with everything I had, swept up by the shivers rushing down my bare arms.

The ballroom doors opened with a bang.

Screams of our guests rang throughout the room. Men shoved women behind them to shield them from the threat. Most of the men in the room aimed their guns at Lorenzo Basile. He strolled down the aisle, his eyes on me, accompanied by a group of men dressed in black suits.

Luca moved me behind him, pressing my chest to his back. My heart beat a million miles per minute. The Knights stood in front of Luca, several rows deep, and had guns in their hands.

Arlo shot up from his chair and moved in front of the Knights. "You're too late, Lorenzo. My son is married to Alexandrea."

Lorenzo strolled toward him, a gun in his hand. "Then I guess I no longer have use for her."

He aimed the gun in my direction but didn't have a clear shot with dozens of men in the way.

Sonny tapped Finn on the shoulder. "Get Mom and Dad out of here."

"Take my parents with you," Drake said.

Finn slipped from the group with Cole at his side. They worked on getting our family members out of the room through the side entrance.

Arlo clutched a gun. "Your issue is with me, Lorenzo. Let's settle this like men."

"Your sons took Alexandrea from my island." He gritted his teeth. "I won her at the auction. I paid thirty million dollars for her, and she is coming home with me."

Arlo pointed his gun at Lorenzo. "As you can see, Alexandrea married my son. She's not going anywhere. Even you know the bonds of marriage are unbreakable in our world."

Lorenzo clicked his tongue. "I don't adhere to silly American rules."

"What is it you want?" Arlo fired back. "Revenge for Eva's death? We didn't kill her. You already know this."

"She was my favorite niece." Lorenzo's face twisted in disgust. "And you ruined her."

"She wanted this life," Arlo said with anger in his tone. "Eva chose me."

"Arlo, hand the girl over." He now had two guns in his hands. "Fight me, and you will all die."

They were about ten feet apart, and their shoulders squared as if they were about to duel. Then, before either of them could shoot, Dante Luciano stormed into the room with Angelo, Stefan, and Nico at his sides. A team of men followed.

"Hello, Uncle," Dante said in a calm, deep tone.

He was gorgeous. He was tall and muscular, with black hair that looked as smooth as silk, styled off his tanned forehead. His cheekbones were high, his lips full. He reminded me of Luca with his demanding presence and Marcello with his athletic build.

Dante was the new head of the Luciano crime family in Atlantic City. They had helped the Knights save me from the island. And according to Luca, he had plotted with Lorenzo's second-in-command to take over the Sicilian family.

Lorenzo's lips parted at the sound of Dante's voice. Then, he spun around and lowered his guns to his sides.

"Here to back me up, Dante? About time."

Dante walked beside his brothers, the four of them a unit. "I came to watch your downfall. The wedding is a sham. Luca and Alexandrea have been married for days." A wicked grin tipped up his mouth. "This is all for show. A ruse to draw you out of hiding. We knew you couldn't resist the challenge of stealing the bride on her wedding day." Dante clicked his tongue. "You're so predictable."

Dozens of men followed Dante, their guns aimed at Lorenzo and his men. Lorenzo was out-manned, outnumbered, and at a complete disadvantage. He had underestimated his opponents. Luca and Marcello had planned out every second of the day and had a backup plan for the backup plan.

Lorenzo tipped his head back and laughed. "You disappoint me, Dante. We had a deal. One day, you could have taken over for me."

His lips curled up into a devious grin. "I spoke with Giovanni Angeli after you offered me his position. It turns out he was eager to replace you. As we speak, he's transitioning into his new role." Dante raised the gun to Lorenzo's head. "Goodbye, Uncle. See you in the afterlife."

And then he pulled the trigger.

Chapter Thirty-Two

ALEX

Hours after the wedding, we arrived at the Salvatore Estate. I stared out the window of the limousine, taking in the breathtaking architecture of my home. This place was once my prison, my worst nightmare, and now I was calling it my home.

I was Mrs. Salvatore.

It still didn't feel real.

If someone had told me I would marry my high school bullies, I would have said they were insane. I never thought I would end up here. With Aiden's help, I thought I would run away and create a new life someplace else.

But I didn't run too far.

Maybe a part of me always knew this was where I belonged. With my family, my broken billionaires.

The loves of my life.

Without a word, Luca grabbed my hand and guided me into the house, leading me upstairs to my bedroom. He didn't speak as he unzipped the dress and slid the straps down my shoulders. I stepped out of the gown, and he handed it to Marcello to hang in my closet. Then Bastian was on his knees, stripping off my garter belt, with Damian working on my other leg.

In a slow, sensual manner, Bastian ripped off one stocking and spread my thighs with his big hands. Damian discarded the other, and his lips were on my inner thigh, planting hot kisses. My skin sizzled from the warmth of their breath, the sensation going straight to my toes.

Marcello stood beside Luca, hands on his narrow hips as he watched his brothers remove every speck of my clothing. Both of their cocks were hard and aimed at me through their slacks. I licked my lips, keeping my gaze on them as I shoved my hands through Damian and Bastian's hair.

They kissed their way up each of my thighs. When they reached my soaking wet pussy, they lifted their heads. Looked up at me with their lips parted, their eyes filled with lust. And then they rolled their tongues over my clit, kissing each other with each flick, and I cried out for them. I loved that they were into each other, even if Bastian tried to deny it.

He thought liking Damian made him gay or bi or put a label on him. I didn't see it that way. Neither did Damian. They could love each other, want each other, and still have me. The three of us could be together without barriers or limits, a judgment-free zone that belonged to us.

Luca tugged on his tie, his gaze unwavering, watching every second of my pleasure. He loved seeing me get off, even if he wasn't the one making me come. I moaned their names, holding onto Damian and Bastian as an earth-shattering orgasm swept through me like a storm.

Luca stroked his monster cock, his movements getting rougher with each tug. Beside him, Marcello gripped his shaft, using the pre-cum to stroke himself.

Luca stepped toward me, smirking. "Get on the bed, Mrs. Salvatore."

Bastian and Damian rose to their full height, quickly removing their suits as Luca pushed me onto the mattress. He pinned my arms above my head and kissed me. His tongue swept into my mouth with a delicious fury, claiming me like he wanted to brand me with his sinful touch.

"Let's play a game."

I grinned at his suggestion. "What kind of game?"

"One you will like." He kissed my lips. "One where you'll come more times than you can count."

"I like this game already."

He glanced over at Marcello, a silent exchange occurring between them.

And then the lights went out.

"Luca." I shifted my weight beneath him. "What kind of game are we playing?"

"I already told you, Drea." His lips moved up and down my jaw and then down my neck. "Do you remember your first time?"

"Of course," I whimpered between kisses. "How could I ever forget that night?"

"Can you tell us apart now?" Luca asked with laughter in his tone.

"Yes," I breathed.

"Let's find out."

His brothers climbed onto the bed with us, each touching me in different places. My heart crashed into my chest, beating so hard and fast I wondered if they could hear the effect they had on me. This time, I wasn't afraid of the unknown. I knew what to expect from my men and welcomed it.

Luca slid off me, and then the four of them shuffled around until I wasn't sure where Luca went. Six months ago, I was terrified of the dark. But my men lived in the darkness and helped me embrace it.

Tracing my fingers over their arms and chests, I felt my way from one to the other. The scent of bergamot filled my nostrils.

I smiled as I touched him. "Bash." Then I moved my hand over the X scar on his chest with the pads of my fingers.

Next, I moved to my left, drinking the scent of Marcello's citrus aftershave. His arms were the thickest, corded with muscle. Even with both hands wrapped around his arm, I couldn't give him a good squeeze.

"Marcello," I whispered.

He leaned forward, clutched my chin, and kissed my lips. "Good girl."

The guys moved around again, leaving me at the mercy of my senses. Kneeling on the bed between them, I felt each of their chests and arms. Luca and Damian were the leanest and the tallest. I knew I had one of them in front of me. They both had scars on their torsos and backs, so that didn't help me navigate their bodies.

But as I continued my exploration, I focused on his scent. Sandalwood. Even if I couldn't smell him, the sheer size of his cock would have given him away. Luca was so long I needed both hands to jerk him off.

"Luca." I gave him a few strokes. "Couldn't miss this big dick, now could I?"

Luca smiled against my cheek, breathing on my skin as his fingers wove through my hair. "You want me inside you, baby girl? Splitting you open, stretching out your tight pussy?"

"Yes," I breathed, almost losing all self-control. "But I need to touch Damian first."

He sat back, his hands falling from my body, and I felt my way in the dark again. I knew what to look for with Damian. A woodsy scent tipped up my nose, and then I let my fingers wander down his stomach over the patch of hair that led to his cock.

"Damian." I pressed my lips to his, a quick kiss that left us wanting more. "Found you."

He rubbed the top of my head. "Good Pet."

After I found each of them, the game had just begun. No

longer giving a damn about the darkness, I let my men take control, desperately needing a release. Marcello curled my fingers around his thick cock. He wasn't as long as Luca, but he was big in other ways.

Luca put my hand around him and helped me stroke him hard. Matching Luca's forceful movements, I jerked both of them, loving how they grunted and groaned as I brought them closer to the finish line.

Damian moved to the bed in front of me. He dipped his head between my thighs and dug his long fingers into my ass cheeks. Then, licking me from front to back, he devoured me like he was starving and dying for a taste. Like he wouldn't survive another second if he didn't eat the cum from my pussy.

My screams of pleasure matched those of my men, and it wasn't long before a rush of cold, then heat shot down my arms, taking me to new heights.

"Damian," I choked out, ready to fall over from the sheer force of his tongue. "Oh, my God. Yes, yes… Mmm… Don't stop."

"Come for us, Cherry." Bastian was behind me, shoving the curls off my shoulders so he could plant soft kisses on my neck.

I moaned with each kiss, closing my eyes so I could feel them.

"That's it, good girl." His teeth grazed my hot flesh, and my skin dotted with bumps of desire. "Come all over my brother's face."

As if on command, my legs trembled, forcing Damian to hold me tighter. I thought Luca would come in my hand like his brother, but he peeled my fingers from his cock. And then he had me on my back, his muscular body pinning me to the mattress. He pushed inside me without warning, breaking through my inner walls in one quick thrust.

Marcello massaged my breast while Bastian's teeth pierced

my nipple, tugging on it like an animal. Throughout my pregnancy, the tiny buds had been sore, but as he bit and sucked, the pain instantly turned to pleasure.

Luca wasn't gentle. Quite the opposite. It still hurt the first time he entered me, even after all these months. He was just too damn big, and I was still so tight.

This time was different.

I knew who was inside me, fucking me, sucking on my nipple, kissing my lips. Each of them found a groove, working in unison to make me come.

Leaning forward, Luca bit my bottom lip. "Scream my name, baby."

"Luca," I moaned and then rattled off their names.

He breathed on my earlobe, grunting with each thrust, taking what he wanted from me. And then Damian reached between us and rubbed my clit with his thumb. Marcello kissed me, parting my lips with his tongue, as Bastian continued sucking on my nipples.

A shiver ripped through my body. Then, one after the other, I came for them, and Luca captured each scream with a kiss.

After Luca came inside me, Damian pushed him out of the way. My sexy prince gripped my hips and then flipped me so he could enter me from behind. He fucked me without mercy, his rough and quick movements wild and out of control.

Bastian tugged on my hair and pushed his cock past my lips. I swirled my tongue around the tip, inching him into my mouth, preparing myself for his size. His hand fell to the back of my head, his fingers roaming through my curls.

Damian fucked me like a possessed psycho, his fingers and cock marking me with each thrust. His hand came down hard on my ass. Once, twice, and then a third whack had me begging for more. I lost myself to the mixture of pain and pleasure, allowing my handsome devils to drag me straight to Hell with them.

Bastian's cum coated my tongue. I swallowed him down, his cock still in my mouth, when Damian came into my pussy.

Saving himself for last, Marcello laid on his back and moved me on top of him. I rode him into the mattress, pressing my palms to his chest, branding his skin with my nails. He didn't seem to mind and slammed into me, taking me harder. None of them treated me like I was breakable.

The five of us fit together perfectly.

And by the time Marcello was coming inside me, exhaustion swept over me, tired from the day's events. So overwhelmed by all the orgasms that my body felt numb.

Marcello snaked his arm around my middle and lowered me to the mattress. Covered in sweat, I lay beside him, with Bastian on my right. I held their hands, needing to feel them.

"I love you guys," I whispered, and Marcello moved his hand to my stomach. "But we can't do this when I get bigger."

"Can't handle us anymore, Cherry?" Bastian laughed. "Are we too much for you?"

"I'm tired all the time." I blew out a deep breath through my nose. "And my stomach is growing. At one point, I was afraid I would tip over."

"You've only gained twenty pounds," Luca pointed out. "That's nothing."

"It doesn't feel the same," I told him. "I have so many aches and pains. And the heartburn… and just so many damn things."

"You're having Damian's baby." Marcello laughed. "It's probably a demon."

Everyone laughed, except for Damian.

"Dickheads," he muttered. "There's nothing wrong with the baby."

My eyelids fluttered, despite my best efforts to fight the

exhaustion washing over me. If they let me, I would have slept for days. But not that easy to do with the baby waking me.

I turned to the side and rested my head on Bastian's shoulder. Marcello rolled over and wrapped his arm around me, making me feel safe and loved.

He brushed the hair off my forehead and kissed me. "Sweet dreams, my beautiful wife."

Chapter Thirty-Three

ALEX

Two months after the wedding, our lives were finally returning to normal. All the guys seemed less on edge. We could leave the house without looking over our shoulders. They were slipping into their roles as husbands and fathers, pampering and showering me with love and gifts.

"I have a surprise for you," Damian said as he led me down the second-floor hallway.

"You've been keeping secrets from me?"

"Not exactly," he said with a devious grin. "I wanted this to be a surprise."

When he opened the door across from my bedroom, I raised my hands in front of my mouth. "Oh, my God, Damian."

I was pregnant with a girl. My dreams and suspicions were one hundred percent true. Call it a woman's intuition, but I just knew. Deep in my bones, I felt a baby girl was in my belly.

Damian moved behind me, placing his hands on my shoulders and dipping his head down to brush his lips against my ear. "Do you like it, Pet?"

Three walls had gray and pink wallpaper, with one accent wall hand-painted with a scene from Swan Lake. Odette was mid-air, floating over the lake, dressed in a ballerina costume, surrounded by swans. The artist used a mixture of white, gray, black, and pink paints to match the room.

At the center of the space sat a custom canopy bed. It was dark, metal, and shaped into tree branches. Like it was in the middle of an enchanted forest. Everything about this room was magical. A crib version of the elaborate bed was on the opposite side of the room. The rest of the furniture was white with pink and gray accents.

Double doors, which led to a private patio, sat between two walls of windows. Sunlight streamed through the curtains, bathing the room in a golden glow. A reclining chair was by the window, and I could already see myself rocking our baby girl as a cool breeze blew in from the bay.

I turned to face Damian, my lips parted in surprise, happy tears streaming down my cheeks. "How did you pull this off?"

"I can't take all the credit." He removed a long velvet box from his pocket. "We've been working on this for a long time." Damian put the box in my hand. "I got you something."

I smiled as I flipped open the box, unable to contain my excitement. A diamond choker with at least thirty massive diamonds. The box and the necklace weighed a ton.

He lifted the necklace from the box with an adorable smile, a real one that reached his green eyes. "Turn around."

He brushed the curls off my shoulder and draped the diamonds around my neck. His long fingers grazed my skin as he fastened the clasp, and I tilted my head to the side. Knowing what I wanted, he pressed a soft kiss on my neck, his lips moving up to my jaw.

"Thank you, Damian," I whispered. "This room. The necklace. It's perfect."

"My pretty Pet needed a collar." He smiled against my cheek. "So you never forget who owns you."

"Please," I shot back. "I own you."

"You do," he said in a deep, sexy tone that sent a chill down my arms. "I'm yours."

I let him hold me in his strong arms for a moment before I needed to see his face, to touch his skin. His eyes illuminated as I spun around and hooked my arms around his neck.

"I love you, Damian." I kissed his lips. "Sofia is going to love you, too."

With his hands on my hips, he stared into my eyes. "Sofia?"

I nodded. "I want to name her after your mom. She was smart and strong, and she gave me you."

He blinked a few times, and I could have sworn his eyes were glassy like he was fighting back the tears. His lips touched mine, and we breathed hard, holding each other without kissing.

"I love you." Damian's fingers wove through my curls, pulling my mouth to his. "I love you, Alexandrea Salvatore. You have given me things I never thought I wanted or could have. But most of all, you taught me how to feel again when I thought there wasn't a single thing about me to love."

I kissed him so hard that the air drained from my lungs. He could have stolen my last breath, and I wouldn't have cared because it would have been worth it.

Of all my guys, Damian was the toughest to crack. I thought he would spend the rest of his life hating himself too much to love another person. But he'd always loved Bastian, even more so than himself.

And hearing those words…

It filled me with so much joy my heart swelled with love for him. I moved his hand over my stomach. My body was filling out, the changes more noticeable. I could still wear my usual loose clothing, but I had to swap out form-fitting outfits for new ones. That gave Luca a new task. He enjoyed picking out my wardrobe and dictating my schedule. It made him happy, so I let him do it. Each of my guys took care of me in different ways.

We kissed for what felt like hours before I heard Marcello's voice.

"Do you like the mural?" He walked into the room, dressed in a black suit with a navy blue tie. He looked handsome, his black hair wavy and falling all over the place. I never understood how he could pull off such a messy look while still looking so put together.

"It's brilliant." I moved toward Marcello. "Who did you hire to paint it?"

He smiled. "I painted it."

I glanced at the wall again, noting the detail in Odette and the scenery, and smiled. "Of course you did. You're so talented, Marcello. I wish you would show the world your art."

He shook his head. "It's for our eyes only."

Marcello was just as talented as his mother. He learned everything he knew from the legend.

He hooked his arm behind my back, and my arms were around him. I stood on my tippy toes and pressed a kiss to his lips. "Thank you. It's perfect for Sofia."

"Sofia?" His eyebrows raised, and then he glanced over at Damian. He nodded. "I love it."

"Where are your brothers hiding?"

"We're here," Bastian said as he entered the room with Luca, running a hand through his dark brown hair. He plopped down on the bed, his gaze shifting between us. "You look happy." A smile tugged at his mouth. "Is this what you had in mind for her bedroom?"

"As usual, the four of you have exceeded my expectations."

Luca stole me from Marcello's arms and planted a kiss on my cheek, his hand covering my stomach. He did this every time he touched me. Like he wanted the baby to know he was here for her. "You're glowing, my queen." His lips grazed my cheek. "Pregnancy suits you. I can't wait to put my child inside you."

"You'll all get your turn," I promised, smiling so hard my cheeks hurt. "But that's it. Only four kids."

"What if you have twins?" Luca shoved the curls off my shoulder. "That's a possibility."

"Four pregnancies," I amended.

"How did you paint the room beside mine without me knowing?" I asked Marcello. "A mural of this size would have taken me months."

He flashed a mischievous grin. "I've been working on it since you found out you were pregnant."

"But how did you know it was a girl?"

"I didn't," he tossed back with a smile. "So I painted two rooms."

My eyes widened. "Let me see the other one."

He slipped his fingers between mine and led me out of the room. He opened the door beside it, and we stepped inside. Instead of the pink and gray swan theme, he painted this space to look like a scene from Greek mythology.

A cartoon version of Achilles wore a bronze Corinthian helmet, greaves, a linothorax, and held a shield. He looked like he was flying through a sea of Trojans, swatting his sword at the soldiers. They dropped one by one at the feet of the best Greek warrior.

"Marcello," I muttered, my eyes filled with tears. "This is incredible. Wow!"

"We can save this room for our son." He kissed the top of my head. "I'm glad you like it. Seeing you smile is worth it."

My guys aimed their adorable smiles at me.

I leaned back against Marcello's chest. "She'll be here soon." I rubbed my palm over my stomach and gasped when I felt her kick for the first time. "Ow."

All four were on top of me, asking me what was wrong.

"Put your hands on my stomach," I told them. "Sofia kicked me."

"I felt nothing," Damian said.

"Same," Bastian agreed.

"Wait for it. Maybe she'll do it again."

A minute passed before I felt her kick, harder than the last.

"I felt it," Damian said in disbelief.

Bastian smiled. "Me too."

Luca and Marcello didn't comment. They just grinned like idiots and kept their hands on me.

"I think she likes her new bedroom. And I think she likes the sound of your voices."

They each took turns getting on their knees and speaking to my stomach like she could talk back. Each time one of them addressed her by name, I felt her move.

I'd never seen Damian look so happy. For the first time in his life, he felt wanted and loved. I ran my fingers through his black hair, and he looked up at me like his world had started and ended with me.

I love you, I mouthed.

Of all my men, he needed to hear it most. He needed the reminder he was worth loving. And I knew his daughter would love him even more than me.

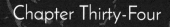

Chapter Thirty-Four

ALEX

We held Evangeline Franco's fifteenth-anniversary gala at the Salvatore Estate. Several hundred people gathered in the main ballroom, their eyes aimed at the stage. My paintings hung around the room, on display for everyone to see. Evangeline Franco's original paintings were beside my recreations, and even Arlo said the similarities were uncanny.

He smiled for once.

I'd never seen that man do more than smirk or scowl, and I brought a smile to his face. Luca was practically glowing. So was Marcello. They were so in awe, shocked by how much I could mirror the techniques of their mother.

Standing on stage beside Madeline Laveau, I looked out into the crowd, my heart pounding. I was ready to burst, my stomach so big I waddled when I walked. But my men seemed even more attracted to me.

After months of putting my heart and soul into Evangeline Franco's recreations, the fifteenth-anniversary show was a smashing success. We raised over a hundred million dollars for the Franco Foundation with my paintings. Art collectors from around the world were in attendance. All of them offered to showcase my Devil-themed paintings in their galleries.

I had to focus on Sofia for now. She was my number one priority at the moment and was nine days late. That was the reason we moved the gala to the estate. With my birthing suite upstairs and my OBGYN on standby, we couldn't risk traveling too far from Devil's Creek.

Luca clutched my hand, with his father on his right. Marcello, Damian, and Bastian were beside him. In public, we had to maintain the illusion I was married only to Luca. Our families were too high profile to risk anyone finding out I was married to all four of them.

They were my soulmates.

My savage Knights.

Madeline gripped the microphone. She waited for the crowd to die down before she spoke. "Evangeline was a dear friend and colleague. We learned a lot from each other. Sold out shows together. Eva will always be in here." She patted her heart. "I think about her every day. She left an indelible mark on the world, touched millions of lives around the globe."

A round of applause rang throughout the room. People raised their glasses to the legend. Well, two legends. Madeline was, in her own right, well-renowned and a brilliant painter.

"It has truly been my honor to serve as the director of the Franco Foundation," she continued with a hint of sadness in her tone. "At the end of the year, I'm passing the torch to a rising star in the art world." Her gaze drifted to me. "I couldn't be more thrilled to have someone so talented run this incredible foundation." She extended her hand to me. "Ladies and gentlemen, please join me in giving a well-deserved round of applause to Alexandrea Salvatore. The next director of the Franco Foundation."

When Luca saw his mother's completed collection, he offered me the job. Not because I was his wife. I could see it in his eyes. He believed I deserved this honor. Of course, I had my doubts. But he convinced me I could still be a solo artist while running the foundation and being a wife and mother.

I could do it all because I had the love and support of four extraordinary men. They made me feel like I could do anything. So I accepted the position when Madeline offered it. She wanted to retire in Barcelona, and it was time for a new era to take over.

I took the microphone from her hand and blew out a deep breath as I stared into the expanse of the room. Hands raised to toast me. People clapped. Some people even whistled.

I smiled so wide my cheeks hurt.

Because I took a chance on my husbands, I had everything I wanted. I wouldn't have been standing on stage without them. They made all the good things in my life possible.

Something wet splashed my feet as I brought the microphone to my lips. I thought someone threw champagne at me until I looked down and saw the puddle of liquid.

My eyes shot toward my men. "I think my water just broke."

I didn't realize I said that into the microphone. Another echo of applause filled the room.

"I'm sorry," I told our guests. "I had a speech planned. But the short version is that I'm so honored to be the new director of the Franco Foundation. Evangeline inspired my art. I learned how to paint by studying her work." Rubbing my hand over my massive baby bump, I added, "I wish I could say more, but it's time to have this baby."

Luca rushed over to me. He put the microphone back in the holder and helped me down the stairs. Marcello, Damian, and Bastian were behind us.

As we left the room, I heard Arlo's voice over the speakers. He would have to close out the night without us.

It was time to meet our little girl.

Chapter Thirty-Five

DAMIAN

My daughter was almost here. It still didn't seem real that after all the horrible shit I'd done, the universe would reward me with a beautiful wife and daughter. I didn't deserve either of them. But Alex made me believe I did, and that was all that mattered.

I finally caved after Luca gave me shit over not reading the baby books. I devoured every single word. Knowing all the possibilities of what could go wrong only made me more nervous. So I hated him for making me read them. But I was also thankful for him and everything he had done to help us prepare.

After months of planning, I could do this. At least, that was what I told myself. Dr. Lansing said this was a step in the right direction for me. That having a child would change me in ways I least expected. Alex put all of her faith in me—a fucking cold-blooded killer—so I figured I must have done something right.

All of us gathered in Alex's birthing room. I stood beside the hospital bed and held her hand. Her entire body trembled, and she squeezed my hand. I brushed the sweaty curls off her forehead, telling Alex she was doing great.

Teeth clenched, she looked up at me, tears streaming down her cheeks, writhing in pain. I wished I could take it from her. Allow her pain to consume me so she wouldn't have to feel anything.

"Almost there." Dr. Ferguson was between Alex's legs. "Push."

A few seconds later, screams filled the room.

Dr. Ferguson held up my daughter. She was beautiful and tiny, with black hair and Alex's blue eyes. The perfect combination of us. So precious and pure, untainted by our world. At this moment, I knew I would do anything to protect her. I would kill anyone who even looked at her.

She was mine.

After the doctor cut the umbilical cord and the nurse cleaned her up, she wrapped Sofia in a blanket and handed her to Alex.

"Hello, Sofia Salvatore." Alex pressed a kiss to her cheek. "I dreamed about you. And you're even prettier than I had imagined. You look just like your daddy."

I leaned down and kissed Alex's forehead, unable to take my eyes off Sofia. Something wet my cheek. I looked up to see if we had a hole in the ceiling because there was no fucking way I was crying. I hadn't done that since the first night I lived with Fitzy.

She swiped at the single tear streaming down my cheek and smiled. "It's okay to feel things, Damian," she said in a hushed tone. "You don't have to be afraid anymore. We're not going anywhere."

I loved her, something I never thought was possible. But maybe I loved her, even when I didn't understand the word's meaning. I'd gotten her name tattooed over my heart years ago. But, in my mind, it was nothing more than an obsession. She was my pet, my pretty little plaything, and I was like a cat hunting a mouse.

For a long time, I had feared she was like Evangeline. I

was terrified she would see the real me and try to push me aside, separate me from my family. But the opposite happened. She brought all four of us closer.

Bastian moved across the room and put his hand on my shoulder. "She's beautiful, D. Congrats."

I angled my body so I could pull him into a hug. He didn't judge me for the tears that wet his shirt. Fifteen years was a long time without feeling human.

We were more than brothers, bound by our trauma and past tragedies. I wouldn't have made it this long without him. Bastian always put me before himself, like he was my father instead of my best friend, my brother.

It was time for me to stop relying on him so much. So I learned how to deal with my dark desires in other ways. Our lives had been pretty quiet since Dante Luciano killed Lorenzo Basile. We had new partnerships, more Knights admitted into the organization, and a new army of men to defend our legacies.

Luca hugged me next, patting me on the back. "You'll do just fine, D. One day at a time, as we talked about, okay?"

I nodded. "Yeah. I got this."

"Congrats, bro." Marcello gave me a one-arm hug and tucked a Cuban cigar behind my ear. "For later."

I smirked. "I doubt we'll be getting any sleep for a while."

He nodded. "But it will be worth it."

Alex looked up at me, her eyelids fluttering. "Damian, do you want to hold your daughter?"

My hands trembled as I took her from Alex.

Luca noticed my uncertainty and was at my side, adjusting her so we were both comfortable. "Like this. Same as the baby books."

"Doing it is not the same as reading about it."

He snickered. "How do you think I learned?"

"Hi, baby girl." Sofia's tiny pink lips curled up into a smile at the sound of my voice. I brushed the soft black hair on her head with my fingers. She was so small and fragile, so damn perfect. "You look just like your grandmother." I kissed her forehead. "She would have loved you, Sofia."

My mom died when she wasn't much older than me. But there wasn't a day I didn't think about her. She was always with me. And even when I was doing bad shit, I wondered if she was watching over me.

I loved Alex even more for naming our daughter after my mom. It meant more to me than she could comprehend.

My gaze shifted to Alex.

Her cheeks were flushed, sweat dotting her skin.

Our girl was beautiful.

I didn't realize something was missing from my life until Alex filled that void. It turns out she was the one person I needed the most.

As I held our daughter, I slipped my fingers between Alex's. She glanced up at me with a tired but happy expression on her face. I mouthed I love you, something she often did to remind me I was worth loving.

Chapter Thirty-Six

BASTIAN

A few months after I killed my grandfather, I received a call from his attorney. The old bastard had left me something in his will. No one knew exactly how much he was worth. He'd hid money in offshore accounts and had shady business affairs.

Alex had never been to The Hamptons, and it was Sofia's first time seeing the beach. We spent the weekend at our house in Southampton, which wasn't far from my grandfather's house in Sagaponack.

The last time I was at his house, Damian couldn't speak, traumatized from the past.

Every time we came back here, it dredged up all the bad memories. But this time, it didn't feel the same. Because taking his life gave us back pieces of ourselves.

The heirs gathered in the ballroom. Two dozen of us sat on wooden chairs facing the front of the room. Mr. Bollinger, my grandfather's attorney, stood in front of a podium with a microphone raised to his mouth.

Alex sat between Damian and me, with Sofia on her lap, bouncing the baby on her knee to keep her from crying. Our daughter looked just like Damian, with black hair and pale skin, her blue eyes as big and wide as her mother.

"Thank you all for coming," Mr. Bollinger said. "Before I read the will, Fitzgerald wanted me to give each of his heirs a letter. But he requested you wait to open it until after I call your name."

He lifted a stack of envelopes from the podium. With each name he spoke, someone rose from a chair. I took the envelope from his hand, wondering what the fuck he could have to say to me. We only spoke when necessary when he was alive.

My father sat beside Luca and Marcello on Alex's right side. Even Carl Wellington received an invitation, which made zero sense. Fitzy had Alex kidnapped so that he could get his hands on Wellington's black book. And after seeing the book for ourselves, we understood why men would kill to get their hands on it.

Grace Hale, my cousin on my mother's side, strolled into the room several minutes late. Just like her biological mother, she had long, blonde hair, sun-kissed skin, and big blue eyes. She walked down the aisle with Cole Marshall.

Grace waved, a gesture I returned as they sat a few rows behind us.

We didn't need to use Grace anymore to trade for a meeting with The Lucaya Group. Everything we'd thought about our parents and their deaths was a lie.

I turned toward the front of the room, waiting for Mr. Bollinger to continue. Alex tapped her fingers on my hand and gave me a reassuring smile. This woman could make even the darkest days seem bright. Every time I looked at her, I wondered how I could live long enough to deserve her.

Mr. Bollinger read the will, rattling off the names of my grandfather's business partners. He divided the shares in each company between them. I had expected the old man to cut all of us out of his will. Do some crazy shit like leave it to charity or someone he didn't even know to spite us.

When Mr. Bollinger got to Carl Wellington, his eyes widened, cheeks reddening as he said, "To Carl, I leave my late wife's vibrator so you can go fuck yourself."

Gasps echoed throughout the room. Most people had too much class or decency to laugh. Carl was furious, but fuck if I didn't want to burst into a fit of laughter.

"To my dear friend, Arlo," Mr. Bollinger continued, "I leave my shares in Atlantic Airlines."

As usual, my father remained expressionless, as if he'd inherited a penny. The stock was worth upwards of two hundred million dollars. I was dying to know what was in his letter. Why didn't he leave the stock to me?

It was our company. Damian should have gotten half of those shares. Or, at the very least, he could have left them in a trust for my future heirs.

"To Damian, I leave you the contents of my basement."

Alex lifted an eyebrow, hoping for an explanation. Damian clenched his hands into fists, his anger shaking through him. Even before he opened the letter, which he read with gritted teeth, he knew what Fitzy had left him.

He handed me the note.

My hand shook as I read the letter, crumbling it in my hand. "That fucking bastard!"

Dirty. Disgusting. Animal.

He had repeated those words to Damian every day for the month he kept us locked in his basement. Damian wasn't right in the head before our parents died. But after our time in this house, he completely fucking lost it.

Monsters are made, not born.

My grandfather left Damian the chains he used to shackle us to the wall. I knew it without stepping foot into the basement. Thinking about those days when we sat in our piss and filth twisted my stomach into knots. If it were possible to resurrect him, I would have dug him up, so I could find new ways to kill him.

I slid my arm across the back of Alex's neck and tapped Damian on the shoulder. "Don't let him get in your head," I whispered. "You're not that boy anymore."

Alex gave me a perplexed look.

I shook my head, giving her a warning look not to push the subject. Not right now. It would have to wait until Damian had time to process, and we weren't sitting in a crowd of people who didn't know about Damian's issues.

"To my grandson, Bastian, I leave my home in Sagaponack and its contents."

As Mr. Bollinger moved on to the next person on the list, I ripped open the envelope.

You are my greatest disappointment.

His letter wasn't much of a surprise. He often told me I hadn't turned out the way he'd wanted, mostly because I wasn't like him. I couldn't believe he left me anything, let alone his precious house, which included his art.

My grandfather loved this place.

There wasn't anything else in the world he loved more, not unless you counted the money. He sure as fuck didn't love me.

"To my granddaughter, Grace," Mr. Bollinger said, snapping me out of my thoughts. "I leave the rest of my estate."

Grace gasped. "Excuse me?"

I glanced over my shoulder at her. She had her hand raised in the air like we were in school. Everyone started at Grace.

"Yes?" Mr. Bollinger said.

"Are you sure the will is valid?" Grace bit the inside of her cheek. "It's just… I don't understand why…" She was so stunned she couldn't get out the words.

"Yes," Mr. Bollinger replied. "Mr. Adams amended the will one month before his death."

"Exactly how much money is the rest of his estate?" Grace asked, her voice shaking.

She'd lived a life of luxury before we placed her into the

care of her adoptive father. A Marine who pretended to be her father for years while teaching her how to survive. Because of him, she was a tough girl and could handle just about anything—even the rigorous cadet training at York Military Academy.

For most of her life, Grace lived on military bases worldwide. She never even owned a laptop until she attended the academy. Overnight, she went from nothing to a billionaire. A true rags to riches story. The real-life Cinderella.

Mr. Bollinger flipped through a few pages on the podium. "Including Mr. Adams' houses, cars, jewelry, stock, bank accounts, and miscellaneous possessions..." He double-checked the figure again and then looked up at her. "Approximately two hundred and fifty-seven billion dollars."

A stifled scream ripped from her throat. "No." She shook her head in disbelief. "That's too much money. He didn't even like me... And I don't want it."

"Grace." I raised my hand to gain her attention. "You deserve it. Take the money, or one of my shitty family members will."

A few of said family members snickered.

Some gave me nasty looks.

Fuck them.

They all had their hands out when I was a child, offering to take me for the money. But none of them wanted Damian. And that was a deal-breaker.

Grace pressed her lips together and nodded. Cole hooked one arm around her, pulling her closer, his head lowered to whisper into her ear.

After Mr. Bollinger read the will, everyone left the house, except for my immediate family and a few of the Knights. Most of my shithead family members left in a huff. I hated the old man for taunting Damian from the grave.

Throwing my arms around Damian, I hugged him hard

enough to burn my fingerprints on his back. His chin dropped to my shoulder, his arms still at his sides.

"Just fucking hug me back, D. You need this."

We both needed it.

"Forget about him." I patted his back. "He can't hurt us anymore."

Two weeks later, I stood in the circular driveway beside Damian. We stared at my grandfather's mansion—my new house—with gas cans in our hands, watching as the flames spread to each room. I'd never seen Damian smile so much.

It was sick and vicious.

But so was mine.

We dropped the canisters into the rented van. Of course, we removed the art and valuables before we lit the match. Alex was now the proud owner of millions of dollars of Renaissance art. She was so fucking happy when the moving company delivered it to the house. The jewels went into the vault beneath our estate for safekeeping.

"Bash." Damian looked at me with those haunting green eyes that sliced through me. "I'm ready to go home."

I nodded. "Let's go."

As we drove off the property, sirens sounded from a distance. I had disabled the security system, so there would be no proof of our crime. The closest neighbor was down the block and wouldn't have seen us coming. Especially not in a van with an untraceable license plate.

Damian turned on the radio, drowning out the fire engine that passed us on our way out of town. He glanced over at me, a smile on his face. He looked like he was finally at peace for the first time in years.

"We're free." I tapped my fingers on the steering wheel. "It's all over, D."

Epilogue

LUCA

One year later

O ur lives had finally settled enough for us to take a much-needed vacation. A late wedding gift from our Sicilian friends. A token of their appreciation for risking our lives to help take down Lorenzo Basile.

With a new baby and Alex's responsibilities to the Franco Foundation, we hadn't had the time to take a honeymoon. Alex wanted to wait until Sofia was sleeping well enough that her nanny could watch her while we were gone for a week.

We were at the Apostolic Palace in Vatican City. The last stop before we left for Sicily. From the time they opened, we toured the Vatican Museums, leaving the Sistine Chapel for last.

Alex walked between Marcello and me, holding our hands, staring up at the ceiling in awe. Her mouth hung open as she noted every detail of the fresco. The ceiling of the Sistine Chapel was a work of art, the highlight of Vatican City.

My mother had spent years studying Michelangelo so that she could paint her fresco. For seven years, she had plaster in

217

her hair, paint and chemicals on her skin. And she loved every moment. Some of my favorite childhood memories were of her standing on a scaffolding ladder with a paintbrush in hand.

She looked so peaceful and in her element. I often thought about her when I watched Alex paint. It was as if the universe had taken my mother from me, only to give me someone like her. So special and unique. I didn't deserve either of them. And yet they both loved me, even after seeing the darkness in my soul, which only made me love them more.

"I wish Mom were here with us," Marcello said as if he could read my mind.

"Me, too," I muttered.

Our children wouldn't have grandmothers, only grandfathers. Not unless we counted Blair Wellington, which we didn't. She was even worse than Savanna.

"I can see how much Michelangelo inspired your mom's fresco." Alex pointed her finger at one pendentive. "Stunning. Your mom nailed the essence of his work."

After she'd explained the meaning behind my mother's fresco, I spent a lot of time in her studio to see if she was right. Of course, she understood my mother. They were so much alike and yet different in so many ways. It was the first time I related to her.

"We need to leave soon," I told her. "The chapel closes in twenty minutes."

She turned her head to look at me, a frown in place. "I'm going to miss it here. But I miss Sofia even more."

"I can't wait to get home," Damian chimed. "Adriana keeps sending me videos of Sofia. She keeps asking for me."

Her face brightened. "She loves her daddy." Then she looked at each of us. "All of her daddies."

I hired Adriana to help us with Sofia right after Alex gave birth. She had postpartum depression and could barely get out of bed, let alone bond with the baby. And even after reading the baby books, Damian still didn't know what he was doing.

Watching him change a diaper for the first time gave me fucking anxiety. So I hired a highly recommended nanny with years of children experience. Even my father took a liking to Adriana, which surprised the hell out of me. He finally seemed open to the possibility of moving on with someone who wasn't my mother. And I was okay with it.

"It's a miracle we can step inside this place without setting it on fire," Bastian joked. He slapped Damian on the back. "Especially this one. He's beyond prayers."

Damian shook his head and laughed. "God must think I'm worth saving, or he wouldn't have given me Alex and Sofia."

Bastian nodded in agreement.

We stood outside once we left the chapel and took in the scenery one last time. I rubbed my hand over Alex's belly. She got pregnant immediately after Sofia. And now, she was having my twin boys.

"I want to name them Leonardo and Michelangelo," Alex said softly, covering my hand on her baby bump. "I have a feeling our boys will be just as legendary."

"Damn right, baby." I kissed her cheek. "Salvatore men are born to rule the world."

She giggled, then kissed my lips. "You're such a cocky asshole. But I love it."

"The names are perfect," Marcello interjected.

Bastian raised an eyebrow. "Leo and Michael?"

"As far as nicknames go," Alex added, "I'm thinking Angelo for Michelangelo."

"Our great grandfather was Angelo," I told her. "We also have a cousin named Angelo. You met him."

She nodded. "Yeah, Angelo Luciano. The twin with the scar on his cheek. So what do you think?"

"I love the names for our boys."

"Time to go." Marcello raised his wrist and pointed at the Chopard watch. "Our ride will be here in five."

♕

Naked and gorgeous, with my babies in her perfect belly, Alex sat on the table and spread her thighs. We hadn't left the villa in Calabria since we arrived last night. Eating and sleeping didn't seem as important when we had our girl all to ourselves. Of course, we loved being fathers, but it was a nice break before the twins arrived.

Since we were all hungry, we cleared off the dining room table and made Alex our meal. Bastian drizzled chocolate syrup on her tits and then rolled his tongue over her nipple. Then he poured some down her stomach so Damian could lap it up. Marcello fed Alex raspberry sorbet, letting some of it slide down to her chin so he could lick it from her skin.

From the moment her cravings started, Alex wanted sugar all the time. I warned her about the dangers of eating junk food throughout her pregnancy, but she was the queen of our corrupt empire. And she got whatever she wanted.

My brothers devoured her, tasting every inch of her delicious body. A soft moan slipped past her lips as her eyes met mine.

She reached between us and fisted my cock. "Fuck me, Luca. I need you inside me."

I smirked. "Patience, my queen."

"Don't make me beg."

I moved between her thighs. "I love when you beg me to come."

My beautiful wife rocked her hips, panting like she was in heat. Massaging her nipple with the pad of my thumb, I pushed inside her. She squealed when I pinched the tiny bud between my fingers as my brothers kissed her from mouth to stomach.

I pumped into her, taking my sweet ass time worshiping her body, making sure she felt every bit our queen. Alex bucked her hips with each bite on her nipples, and her moans turned into screams. My little devil begged us for more as her entire body trembled, riding out another earth-shattering orgasm.

After I finished inside her, she gave me a sexy smile, which I returned. That was something I did more often. Alex gave me a sense of peace, even in times of war. She was the cure for my madness, the angel on my shoulder when I wanted to do nothing but sin.

My pretty, broken girl pieced me back together. She gave me a dreamy look like she couldn't believe I was hers when I couldn't believe she was mine.

Ours.

I pulled out of her, and our cum dripped down her thighs. She blew out a few deep breaths with her palm over her heart.

I traced my fingers up her stomach. "You okay, Mrs. Salvatore?"

She looked at me. "Never better."

"How about Leo?" I slid my hand to her belly. "And Angelo. Are they kicking again?"

"Not right now."

Ours sons were growing inside her. One of them would be the next Grand Master of The Devil's Knights. The heir to the Salvatore and Wellington fortunes. Our sons would be kings among men, the rulers of two of the largest empires in the world.

Alex was eight weeks from her delivery date. This was our last chance to leave Devil's Creek before birth.

I swiped my thumb across her sexy lips. "You're such a good wife."

O n our last day in Italy, we drove through the coastal town of Calabria with the convertible top down. The wind whipped through Alex's blonde curls as we rode into the mountains. She looked more beautiful than ever, wearing a pale blue strapless dress that inched up her tanned thighs.

Alex glanced over at me, a smile stretching across her beautiful lips. "Are we going to the beach?"

I lifted her hand from the center console and kissed her skin. "Not this one."

"What's wrong with this one?"

"Nothing," Marcello interjected. "We'll have more privacy where we're going."

She smiled. "I want to make love to all of you on the beach."

"Whatever you want, boss lady," Bastian joked.

"We'll be there soon." I patted her knee. "My parents took us to this beach when we were kids."

"I could see your mom sketching on the beach."

I gripped the steering wheel, taking the turn slow. "Maybe you'll come up with your next Devil-themed painting while we're here."

"I hope so." She sighed. "I have another exhibition in two months. I'm five paintings short and have pregnancy brain."

"You can use me as your inspiration." Damian gripped the headrest, leaning over to speak in her ear. "I love being your muse."

She reached behind her and touched his hand. "The Devil I Fear." Then she tapped my hand. "The Devil I Hate." Her eyes moved to the back, landing on Bastian. "The Devil I Love." She saved Marcello for last, her face illuminated with a smile. "The Devil I Crave."

Art collectors had reached out, offering as much as fifty million dollars for the four paintings of us. No one would ever see the originals. Not as long as I was alive. We bought them from Alex's first showing to ensure no one would ever have pieces of us that belonged in our home, not a gallery.

Because of Alex, we no longer feared love. Even Damian had gotten over his belief that he was unworthy of it. All four of us placed our black hearts in her hand, knowing she would care for them.

When we arrived at our destination, I led Alex by the hand to the beach. Marcello carried the basket while Bastian and Damian gathered the beach chairs and bags from the trunk.

Caminia had a smaller, less developed beach than those in Calabria, but I liked this one best. Hidden by rocky cliffs, we had complete privacy from the outside world. Giovanni Angeli had assured us we would have the beach to ourselves for the rest of the day.

I laid down a blanket, and Marcello set the basket on the sand. We sat beside our wife, who stared into the expanse of the water, a huge smile plastered on her beautiful face.

"Wow, I can't believe no one is here."

"I told you we'd have privacy."

She looked at me. "What did you do?"

I rolled my shoulders. "Nothing. But Giovanni may have had something to do with the lack of people on the beach."

Alex rifled through the basket's contents, uncapped a water bottle, and took a swig. I moved her between my thighs and rubbed my hand over her stomach.

Alex leaned back against my chest. "This is perfect. Thank you for arranging our trip." She moved her hand over mine. "It's a shame we have to live like this, always watching over our backs. When we return to Devil's Creek, I'm not leaving the estate until you find out who's trying to kill Drake."

"I won't let anything happen to you," Marcello promised, slipping his fingers between hers.

Bastian moved between Alex's thighs and shoved her panties to the side, sliding his finger up and down her wet slit.

He licked his lips as he pushed inside her. "You look so beautiful right now, Cherry." My brother put his hand on her stomach and pumped his fingers into her. "I love seeing you pregnant with our babies."

She moaned as he withdrew his fingers and plunged into her once more. "I can't wait to have all of your children."

"I'm putting my baby in you next," he said with mischief in his gray eyes.

"No, you're not," Marcello fired back. "I was supposed to get the first child. All of you assholes got what you wanted but me."

"You got me," Alex said in a singsong tone.

"Yeah, princess, I did." He kissed her lips as Bastian fingered her. "But my brothers made promises. Bash got your virginity. Luca got to marry you. Damian wanted to be the first to claim your ass. And I wanted to get you pregnant."

She moaned into his mouth. "You'll have your chance, Marcello. You're next. Okay?"

Bastian groaned but didn't complain. We owed Marcello after fucking him over, ignoring his only request with Alex. But fuck, how could any of us pull out when she felt so damn good?

After she came, Alex climbed onto Bastian's lap, sucking his bottom lip into her mouth. He stripped off his shirt, and then he worked on removing her sundress. They were both naked and panting, breathless, as Bastian lifted her onto his cock.

Alex cried out as he stretched out her pussy. "Go slow, Bash. I can't handle the roughness." She clutched his shoulders, her eyes moving between us. "Make love to me."

He bounced her up and down on his cock, taking his time.

"Come for me, Cherry."

She moaned his name and whispered that she loved him. That she loved all of us. As she was about to come, I reached over and massaged her clit. Our sexy queen unraveled like a ball of yarn.

My cell phone rang, interrupting our moment of perfection. I sighed when I saw Sonny Cormac's name on the screen because I told the Knights not to call while we were in Italy.

"It must be important," Alex said when she saw the Caller ID. "You should get it."

I put the phone on speaker so everyone could hear. "This better be good."

"Drake is gone." Sonny struggled to catch his breath. "The Lucaya Group blew up his lab at Battle Industries."

Alex covered her mouth with her hand and gasped. "No."

"You need to get home," Sonny continued. "You're not safe."

We once thought The Lucaya Group killed Bastian and Damian's parents. It was all a lie. But that still didn't remove the threat. Drake Battle developed an artificial intelligence software that put him on the radar of governments worldwide, terrorist organizations, and even crime syndicates.

Over the past year, we'd had our share of close encounters, dodging constant threats. The group wanted Drake's software, powerful tech that, in the wrong hands, could kill millions of people. That was the reason Drake canceled the program. The beta proved too unstable to release into the world.

"Get home now," Sonny added. "The Knights need their leader." He blew air into the receiver. "There's one more thing… I found a girl in a Mac Corp shipping container. She's the daughter of Cian Doyle."

Marcello took the phone from my hand to talk to his best friend. "Are you fucking kidding me, Son?"

"Afraid not. I left her at the safe house in Beacon Bay."

"Cian Doyle is Declan's enemy," I pointed out. "Why the fuck haven't you handed her over to him?"

Declan O'Shea was Sonny's uncle and an Irish Mob boss. He lived in Beacon Bay and served his purpose occasionally. But Cian was even more powerful, with strong ties to the IRA and other groups that ran guns and drugs.

"Because I'm trying to figure out what she's hiding," Sonny shot back. "I'll deal with the girl. Don't worry about it."

"How old is she?" Bastian asked.

"In her early twenties."

"Figure out what she's hiding, and then get rid of her," I ordered. "Alex is ready to pop out the twins. We don't need another crazy mob boss breathing down our backs."

"I'll handle it," Sonny promised. "It won't blow back on any of you or the Knights."

"It better not," I fired back. "Assemble the local Knights to help look for Drake."

I ended the call.

Alex lowered the sundress over her head and, with Damian's help, rose from the sand. She bit the inside of her cheek, staring up at me. "Should I be scared?"

"We'll get Drake back."

I hope.

I prayed Drake could handle interrogation long enough for us to rescue him. All Knights undergo a rigorous interrogation process during initiation, everything from waterboarding to being burned with a blowtorch.

Not for the faint of heart.

I stroked her cheek with my thumb. "We'll find Drake."

She cocked an eyebrow at me. "Alive?"

I nodded. "That's the goal."

Alex placed our hands on her baby bump as we stared into the expanse of the water. "I wish we could stay here forever."

"Me, too," we whispered in unison.

The Frost Society

Welcome to The Frost Society!

You have been chosen to join an elite secret society for readers who love dark romance books.

When you join The Frost Society, you will get instant access to all of my novels, bonus scenes, and digital content like new-release eBooks and serialized stories. You can also get discounts for my book and merch shop, exclusive book boxes, and so much more.

Learn more at JillianFrost.com

Also by Jillian Frost

Princes of Devil's Creek

Cruel Princes

Vicious Queen

Savage Knights

Battle King

Read the series

Boardwalk Mafia

Boardwalk Kings

Boardwalk Queen

Boardwalk Reign

Read the series

Devil's Creek Standalone Novels

Wicked Union

Read the books

For a complete list of books, visit JillianFrost.com.

About the Author

Jillian Frost is a dark romance author who believes even the villain deserves a happily ever after. When she's not plotting all the ways to disrupt the lives of her characters, you can usually find Jillian by the pool, soaking up the Florida sunshine.

Learn more about Jillian's books at JillianFrost.com

Printed in Great Britain
by Amazon

24271110R00137